!!!L

MW01265061

~~DR. DYE'S~~ HEALING MIRACLE SPRINGS
HUBBARD, ILLINOIS

SITUATED IN THE CENTER OF TOWN IN A PARK CONTAINING NINE ACRES OF GROUND WITH FIVE GROVES OF SUGAR TREES, **GREEN LAWN SPRINGS** ARE THE PROPERTY OF DR. I. WM. DYE, WHO HAS KEPT THEM OPEN FOR HIS PATIENTS AND GENERAL PUBLIC FOR A NUMBER OF YEARS.

THERE ARE A HALF DOZEN OR MORE SPRINGS, THREE OF WHICH HAVE BEEN ESPECIAL FAVORITES OF THE DOCTOR, WHO TESTIFIES TO THEIR MEDICINAL VIRTUES, NOT ONLY FROM HIS OBSERVATION OF THEIR EFFECTS UPON HIS PATIENTS, BUT FROM ITS PERSONAL USE.

CENTRAL SPRINGS ANALYSIS: CARBONATE IRON, BI-CARBONATE SODA, CARBONATE POTASH, CARBONATE LIME, CHLORIDE SODIUM, TRACES OF IODINE, AND SULPHUROUS ACID. THIS ANALYSIS, WHILE IT SHOWS THE GENERAL CHARACTER OF THE WATER, WILL SUGGEST TO THE INTELLIGENT PHYSICIAN THE VARIOUS DISEASES FOR WHICH THESE WATERS MAY BE PROFITABLY AND PROPERLY USED.

THE SPRINGS, SITUATED WITHIN A FEW FEET OF EACH OTHER, BELONG TO THE CLASS KNOWN AS SALINE CHALYBEATE. THE DISEASES FOR WHICH THEY ARE PARTICULARLY SUITED ARE LIVER AND KIDNEY DISEASES, DYSPEPSIA, RHEUMATISM AND GOUT.

ONE OF THEM IS ESPECIALLY VALUABLE IN THE PREVENTION OF THE DISEASES PECULIAR TO CHILDREN DURING THEIR FIRST AND SECOND SUMMERS!!!

DR. I. WM. DYE
GREEN LAWN SPRINGS
715 BUNYAN STREET
HUBBARD, ILLINOIS

(Paid Advertisement)

Also by

Dusty Bracken

asitiswhenitwas [Brick Five, Book/Novel, 2018]

The Bricklayers

"Get a Job" [Brick One, Single, 2012]
The Addiction EP [Brick Two, CD/EP, 2012]
"The Great Debate" [Brick Three, Single, 2013]
Gullible's Travels [Brick Four, CD/LP, 2013]
A History of Whispers [Brick Six, CD/LP, 2018]
The Bricklayers [Brick Seven, CD/LP, 2019]
"Human Condition" [Brick Eight, Single, 2020]
White Fragility [Brick Nine, CD/LP, 2020]
"Would It Kill You to Smile?" [Brick Ten, Single, 2021]*
Octaves and Oligarchies [Brick Eleven, CD/LP, 2021]
Verses [Brick Twelve, Book/Memoir, 2022]
Duality [Brick Thirteen, CD/LP, 2022]
Rebuilt [Brick Fourteen, EP, 2023]
Soundtracks [Brick Fifteen, CD/LP, 2023]

*with Angela French

Here is the House

An Anthology

Dusty Bracken

Brick Sixteen
September, 2006/August, 2018
New Orleans, Louisiana/St. Louis, Missouri/Collinsville, Illinois/
Mt. Vernon, Illinois

For

Little Buddha

and

The Patriarch

ing the physical symptoms of stress and anxiety while the soul takes refuge elsewhere....

My soul built a house that looked, walked, talked and even smelled like me but was, in truth, Dusty Bracken.

Meanwhile, my body became little more than a dreary fire hazard....

✿

The result is the present flimsy collection of detritus, scribbled and scattered in the aftermath of the untimely and unnecessary death of The Woman I Love, reassembled and reassessed these fifteen years later, and every smeary word reading like the work of a relative stranger. Whether it was written by the body I had temporarily escaped or by Dusty Bracken, the memory of having actually sat down and done so is lost to the gargoyles.

Perhaps these stories (each one an appraisal of the universal but profoundly personal experience of loss) exist by virtue of their own will (being a sort of tulpa of my tulpa).

Probably not.

Regardless, they exist.

Apparently, so do I.

Peace.

A Brief History

I. 7th September 2006
II. 7th June 2008
III. 25th September 2008
IV. 21st January 2009
V. May/June 2009
VI. 28th June 2009
VII. June/July 2009
VIII. September 2009/January 2010
IX. January 2010/August 2011
X. 5th January 2010
XI. October 2006/May 2007/September 2008/May 2009

I. "No Regrets, Yeats...No Regrets…"

I had wanted to write something about the flooding of New Orleans -
to add something to the public discussion of the levees,
to bear witness.

But I'm sitting
in a shuttered doorway
on some crowded street
in the French Quarter,
and the Woman I Love has just
rested her head on my shoulder.

The sun is setting behind us,
and a small tree to our right
is vibrating with birdsong.

By accident,
we have arrived
on the weekend of
Southern Decadence -
a celebration of Pride -
so it's an often-fabulous crowd
milling past,
their movement
made perfect
by the mix of
live and pre-recorded music
falling out of open shop doors:

jazz
giving way to
hip-hop
giving way to
zydeco
giving way to
electronica…

He produced a
large, triangular beaker
from inside his left sleeve
and set it down
next to me
as I sat up.

"The nurse is monitoring my output," he said,
pointing to the numbers and hash marks
on the side of the beaker,
"so we have to measure the contents."

"Is your nurse here, too?" I asked.

I got
out of bed
to kneel
on the floor
in front
of him.

"No," he said.
"I decided to take a short walk -
you know, to keep my strength up -
but the movement sometimes stimulates output…
so here I am."

He chuckled as he
lifted the hem of his gown,
revealing the bag and
the open wound it surrounded.

The stoma
was bright
and pink,
and the skin around it
had dutifully shrunk down
to fit it neatly,
like a turtleneck.

He pointed to a nearby scar:
"See, the spear
cut off blood flow
to a section of my bowel,
so the doctor
removed that section,
connected the remaining ends,
then brought a piece of my
small intestine
to the surface
to relieve pressure
on the wound,
and to make it easier
to poop
until I heal," he explained,
which surprised me.

"You can't heal yourself?" I asked.

He shot me
a sideways glance:
"If you don't wanna help me,
I'll ask someone else," he said.
"I just thought you could use the practice."

And he held
out the beaker
for me
to take,
which I did.

Holding the beaker beneath the bag with one hand,
I situated the closed mouth of the bag just inside.

Then,
with the beaker balanced in my lap,
I undid the clip on the bag,
releasing the warm, skunky
contents.

"*Gloop, ploop*," said Jesus's output
as it tumbled south.

"How much you got there?" he asked,
handing me a washcloth
to wipe
the end
of the bag,
which I did,
then clipped it closed again.

In the half-light of the bedroom,
I held up the beaker and read the side of it.

"200 millilitres," I told him,
then rose
to go
flush it.

"I'll take that," he said as he, too,
rose to his feet.

Taking the beaker,
he turned to leave,
thanking me for my help before
stopping at the door to watch me
crawl
back into bed.

"I love you," he said,
and his voice
was suddenly
sweet,
and kind,
and beautiful
in its inflection
as he opened the door
and spoke again:
"I love you."

And it was her voice,
The Woman I Love,
that loved me
back to sleep and
out of my dream and
into the morning when
I awoke and rose to see her again...

...sweet,
and kind,
and beautiful...

...but her weight loss is suddenly obvious –
particularly in her face.

Her bone structure is
formidably classical –
those elevated cheek bones and
strong jaw
crowning
that long neck –
but has never been so prominent.

Her color
comes
and goes
with the return
of her nausea
and her smile
has become
modest.

And the news is hard:
It's not the type of cancer we thought it was…
and it's become aggressive, so we need to begin intensive chemo…
which could complicate her surgical incisions….

She vomits
her liquid supper
into a pink, plastic tub,
wipes her mouth,
then scolds her father
for looking so sad…
but when he's out of the room,
she
breaks
down.

"You'll get dehydrated
if you keep crying like that," I joke,
as if she hasn't spent
the last month
puking her guts up.

She smiles,
wipes her eyes,
and presses the button
on her
morphine pump.

I lean over her
and kiss her resolutely
on the lips,
which are caked
with sputum,
and she
holds me close
for a full minute
of silent eye contact
before flirting,
"Wanna help me empty my bag?"

"You know I do," I smile,
bouncing my eyebrows
before slipping off
to the bathroom
to retrieve
a triangular,
plastic beaker.

When I return,
she is seated
on the edge
of the bed
and wiping her mouth
clean.

I kneel
in front of her
as she lifts her gown
to reveal her ostomy.

Balancing the beaker in my lap,
I place the closed bottom
of the bag
inside,
undo the clip,
and release the contents.

"Thank you," she says
as I clip the bag closed,
then hands me a wash cloth
to wipe clean
the bottom of
the bag.

Another smile: "My pleasure."

Then, rising
to return the beaker
and contents
to the bathroom:

"I love you, you know."

And she answers,
quietly and sweetly,
"No. *I* love *you*."

When I return,
she is sleeping,
and I
can see
her heartbeat
throbbing
in her neck.

III. "Dreams Never End."

Last night,
I slept in our bed
for the first time
in 150 days.

I slept
on your side,
on your pillow –
"the one that you dreamt on."

At about 1.30 a.m.,
one of your dreams woke me,
himself awakened by a dream.

So I went to him,
held him,
and we cried
for want of your love.

IV. "Inauguration Day Gamble."

No work today,
so we get to watch the Oath together.

You are two weeks shy of your second birthday
(give or take a day or three),
squirmy,
and jonesin' for some *Scooby Doo*...

...but the disconnect between
retention and *recollection*
is a largely conscious construct (right?)
and if, in a dream, you are someday able to
locate the residue of this moment –
when the Melting Pot heaved
and a writer took the Oath –
and you hear your father giggle like a lotto winner,
even if it's just
shadows and sounds,
perhaps you'll be glad
I held you here for forty-five seconds
today...

...perhaps you'll only remember
having to wait for *Scooby Doo*...

V. "Humiliation."

His paranoia runs deep – the remnant river of an ancient ocean of fear and superstition – and using the open air washing bay at the Help Urself Car Wash (.75¢ for three minutes) he can feel eyes bearing down on him, sizing him up, taking aim....

He feels exposed, the water wand in his hand, his attention largely devoted to the spotty, green stains that texture the top of his white car (daily, he is forced to park where the branches of his neighbor's black walnut tree hang over the fence so that feeding squirrels are able to sit over the horseless carriage and gingerly drop their rinds, discoloring his car in seemingly random splotches, as if Jackson Pollack himself is in the tree, a paint-soaked, dripping brush clutched in his teeth as he frantically tippy-toes up and down the bouncing branch...)...and the environs are wide open.

Completely vulnerable, he is an easy target with nothing but parking lot separating him from the darkened windows across the street, where the eyes are....

He works his way around so that his back is to the bricks (east), allowing him to easily monitor the rest of the asphalt expanse (north, south, and west), and his hand *tightens* on the water wand, though his distraction has compromised his aim so that he is now absentmindedly washing the rear passenger window cleaner than clean, the streaming rinse obscuring further his son's smiling toddler face as seen through the glass.

"Paranoia will destroya," a college smoking buddy had chimed every time one or the other of them would sneak a peek into the dormitory hallway to look for the Resident Assistant (the same asshole smoking buddy who would always greet a particular Design major – who lived at the end of the hall and who had only recently exited the proverbial "closet" – with a limp-fish handshake and stupid rhyme: "There will always be apod-o-me that just *adores* sodomy.")

Today, however, aged thirty-seven and sober, it's no better....

His eyes transfixed on what he thought was a rustling of the curtains in the kitchen window of the brick home across the street to his left, he doesn't notice the figure emerging on his right, creeping around the brick wall from the next washing bay like a swiftly shifting shadow, sliding slightly toward him, extending its manicured hand, and touching him softly on the shoulder....

"Holy *shit!*" he barks, swivels, then douses the figure from crotch to crown with the same Sur-Kleen soap solution he has just spent a minute and a half spraying at his son's visage.

"Dammit, Ron!" yells the suddenly-frantic figure, throwing its arms up to shield its face and backing away. "Spook much?!"

A pause as Ron recognizes the voice, lowers the spray, and names his victim: "Dr. Burke?"

His therapist.

His Therapist!: Replacing the water wand on its wall mount, he glances briefly at his son, who is laughing uproariously at the display, then quickly moves to close the distance between himself and the headshrinker.

"You can't creep up on me like that," he half-mutters to the soggy psychiatrist, who is the physical doppelganger of Freud himself (though his own approach and philosophy only pay lip-service to the father of psychology, granting credit where credit is due, but otherwise employing "a more *organic* approach to self-revelation, discovery, and disclosure"...whatever that means...). At the moment, however, his arms straight out at his sides, the doctor suddenly resembles an apprehended fugitive suspect, his beard and suit dripping, and Ron lamely "frisking" him in an attempt to brush water from the doctor's clothes with the palms of his hands.

"I thought we'd made progress in that area," Burke mutters back as the water wand on the wall continues to spritz the asphalt beneath with soapy Kleenness.

"*Ffffffssssss*," says the water wand.

"*Schschsch*," says the Sur-Kleen solution as it bubbles up, then slowly resolves itself and finds its way to the drain beneath Ron's car.

Pushing Ron away, the doctor now begins frisking himself, cupping his right hand around his left arm as he slides it from shoulder to cuff, pushing the saturation out of the cloth as if from a chamois.

"Um," says Ron. He began seeing the doctor a year after his wife died, exhausted from "being strong," his perception cloudy and blurred by sadness, and his initiative, his purpose, his *raison d'etre*...his reason to be sits strapped into his car seat and giggling his simple giggle, but, in all honest appraisal, some days even the boy isn't enough to keep him here....

His symptoms: sadness, anxiety, paranoia...

...and The Darkness....

Nailing Ron with the sort of eye contact one might expect only from an iron maiden, the doctor opens his mouth to speak, but stops short...then tries again, speaking quietly but directly, as if the iron maiden has a confession to make: "We will need to address this."

"I'll pay your dry cleaning, too," Ron offers (m)eagerly, but the doctor scoffs softly.

"Stop being so damn jumpy and we'll call it even," he groans, then turns swiftly, creating a spray of daredevil suds leaping from his shoulders and into nothingness.

"I'll see you Thursday," he sputters as a distasteful after-thought before disappearing back around the wall to his washing bay and sports car.

Ron drives his dead wife's Chevy.

VI. "Nostalgia."

It's nice
to be nine years old
in 1983 and
to be jumping up and down
on the couch
in the family room
at a friend's house,
Michael Jackson singing in the corner,
my skinny church friend laughing
because he's just bonked his head
on the ceiling
while my not-so-skinny self
can't quite seem to jump as high,
but who cares –

true self-consciousness won't kick in
until puberty,
and that's an eternity away
when you're nine years old
in 1983 and
everyone you love is alive.

"Did you call 911?"

"No, I mean – "

"Dammit, woman! I'll be right there! Now call 911!")

And so Charlotte Strickt leapt into action – loaded the living room VCR with an old, hour-long documentary about dinosaurs (which never failed to thoroughly mesmerize her daytime ward), double-checked the padlocks on the refrigerator and pantry doors (*locked!*), then quietly slipped out through the back door of the Shiner household and into her car at 3:30 that day...an hour early....

Charlotte's son, Erick, had grown up with Jacob Shiner, living just two houses apart, separated by only three years, attending the same grade school and high school. Now that the boys were older (in-their-fifties older) and worked together, she was proud of the connection she felt she had helped cultivate in her son's early life – a long-term bond that must have surely provided a great deal of solace over a lifetime of daily trials....

Oh, she was very proud – of her son (who was quiet and average), her husband (who built furniture and performed odd jobs for the local gentry), and of the household the three of them had comprised (a pleasant, modest home next to Ridgway's Monument Co. at the corner of Bunyan and Seventeenth streets). At work, Charlotte was the stalwart, the work horse; at home, she was queen and martyr (depending on whether or not she was able to get her way); at church, she was the plain-spoken Sunday School mistress (two generations of Campbellites had thus far realized their faiths under her circumspect tutelage); and in bed, she was the amorous lover (yes, even still – menopause had been a bitch, but it had also liberated her and her spouse from the shackles of birth control, and with the help of lubricants and a strategically-timed medication, the septuagenarian Charlotte and Elwin Strickt were able to have some of the best sex of their little lives).

Such a proud woman – particularly regarding her care and devotion to her older sister, who (as Charlotte perceived) never found love and subsequently lived her life as one full of distractions. But Eleanor Spitsinger was well-traveled, well-educated, thoughtful and independent; she was worldly, but full of such whimsy that one was forgiven for imagining the secret, unshared events of her long and liberated life – no men to dog her heels, to try and change her, to impose expectations (certainly, Charlotte believed only half of what Eleanor *had* shared with her).

It was with the same sense of pride that Charlotte Strickt also charged Jacob Shiner only twenty dollars a day to spend her weekdays watching his son (and cleaning the house) from 6:30 a.m. to 4:30 p.m., while Jacob was at work...where her son also worked...of whom she was *very* proud....

It was Jacob who had gotten Erick the job, in fact. Having been there for six months, Jacob had somehow so endeared himself to the warehouse owner that even with her son's right leg in a cast, the glowing recommendation of Jacob Shiner had gotten Charlotte's boy hired. Now, thirty years later, they were the only employees at the warehouse who had any seniority at all.

But *pride goeth before destruction*, and had she ever stopped to listen to herself some Sunday morning as she shared the words of the Hebrew king, she may very well have paused before leaving her daytime ward to attend her sister....

...and a haughty spirit before a fall...

She just might have paused, considered her situation, weighed potential consequences, chosen wisely, and waited....

The twenty-two year old Andrew Shiner was a tall, obese, autistic manchild who loved dinosaurs, but whose conscious thought processes were largely dominated by what his doctor had identified as *pica* – an apparently insatiable compulsion to put things in his mouth...and not just for sustenance. He would put anything and everything of compatible size into his oral cavity, and his file at the community hospital attested to it: description after description of emergency room visits during which the boy's digestive system was rescued from swallowed batteries, pencils, glass, Tylenol, toothpicks, et cetera. He possessed little self-control, mostly spontaneous reflex, and when he felt the fullness in his ears and sensed the subliminal cricket chirping just behind his left eye, he would (without an instant of hesitation) reach for whatever was close and would fit into his soggy cake hole.

Thus was everything in the Shiner household hidden away, locked up, nailed down, or squirreled into a storage locker across town.

Certainly, everything having to do with Andrew's mother was quite thoroughly hidden away where only Jacob had access....

✿

Anyway: It was Charlotte's car that alerted Andrew to the fact that he was alone.

Riddled with holes, the muffler on Charlotte's chariot muffled about as well as if it had been made entirely out of cheese cloth, and when she twisted her wrist to turn the key the old Plymouth roared to life like a Tyrannosaurus Rex sounding its imperative call for more flesh. A couple taps on the accelerator as Charlotte backed out of the driveway and T. Rex suddenly wasn't just hungry, he was horny, too, roaring the details of his itch to all down the block as the old woman quickly accelerated and steered to the Stop sign, barely complied, then roared left....

And Andrew, at the dining room window, saw it all, the roaring having brought the boy to his feet...and when it began to dawn on him that he may very well be alone...he began to twitch...and his belly *ached*....

"Charlotte?" he muttered, his unbelieving, giddy eyes scanning the room as he turned from the window.

No answer.

Just the video narrator describing the prehistoric landscape over which the dinosaurs had ruled.

Systematically, he went from room to room, scouring the shadows, muttering, twitching, aching, and so, *so hungry*....

"Charlotte?"

No answer.

"Charlotte?"

No answer.

But God *damn* the voice inside of him – pleading, demanding...how sad it made him feel, the compulsion that niggled at his better inclinations, demons trumping angels with blocks of cheese, swords blunted by cupcakes, guns disabled with syrup and strawberries, and...*oh, God*....

Every cabinet in the kitchen was locked...every cabinet...*every fuckin' cabinet – locked, locked, locked!*

He circled the center of the room swiftly, his eyes darting from cabinet to cabinet, sizing up each lock individually, mumbling to himself ("Just a cookie...I'm so hungry...just a cookie…"), ecstatic to be alone, but solely focused on the task at hand: the locks, his hunger, his compulsion, the locks….

He began to cry.

He began to rage.

"Sooo fuckin' hungry...just one God damn cookie..."

He stopped, dead in his tracks, and studied the lock in front of him, narrowing his eyes the way he had seen a T. Rex do as it squinted through near-complete blindness for the prey it had so deftly sniffed out….

This lock, appearing so complete and solid...*this* lock, yielding after only three kicks, was weak...and, okay, so the items beneath the sink weren't really considered food or even at all edible, but such a thirsty boy (who had been *so good* for *so long*) – such a thirsty boy couldn't be expected to go without respite or satisfaction….

Respite: The wetness on his tongue unleashed such a rush of relief that his entire body relaxed in almost pure marionette fashion, the entire 326 pound girth of his six-foot-three-inch frame tipping back to lean against the countertop, which popped its disapproval loudly.

Satisfaction: Though it burned as he swallowed, the lemon aspect of the cleaner brought a smile as wide as the sunrise and seemed to clear his head, as well – the same sensation that had come with every menthol cough drop or smear of vapor rub now spread behind his eyes and in his nose. With a capstone swig that warmed his belly and emptied the bottle, he sniffed the kitchen air, smiling and swelling his chest (*just like* a T. Rex) before stooping again to the chemical larder beneath the sink, from which he retrieved a medium size box of steel wool....

✿

So that's what it was (the rustling of the curtains in the kitchen window across the street from the car wash where Ron stood deriding the world he perceived as hostile): It was Andy Shiner, alone for the first time in ages, collapsing against the wall, the curtains tugged between the boy and the wall as he slid to the floor, gasping and burning, his stomach a-flame with the concentrated ammonia cleaning power of Bauer's Lemon Blast, his windpipe a-bulge, blocked and bleeding with Scrubz pre-soaped steel wool....

VIII. "Condescension."

Once upon a time, Charlotte Strickt's only child was the thoroughly average boy, Erick Strickt.

On the day Andrew Shiner died, he was the thoroughly average man, Erick Strickt – as average a specimen of modest evolution as human DNA can produce in these modern times.

And the perfectly average Erick Strickt turned no heads and stole no hearts; no longing stirred in his wake and even his shadow appeared to pursue him only because it had no choice.

Like the majority of his American, male compatriots in their fifties, he read at a fourth grade level, stood five-foot-nine-inches tall, and believed in God, Satan, and their respective abilities to influence the tangible world. His weight was 165 pounds, fifteen pounds of which were thanks to an average American diet heavy in carbohydrates. Balding, the hair atop his head hung limp and poorly combed while his temples had embraced the "color" gray so enthusiastically that they had practically assumed the silvery hue entirely, though his face remained awkwardly youthful.

His face, awkwardly youthful, was his worst enemy.

That is, because of his youthful gaze (graying temples and thinning dome aside), his peers (who had hardly aged as gracefully) refused to ever take him seriously. His "boss" (Jacob Shiner, who was only just enough above average to be able to bullshit his way into positions of perceived authority) would talk to Erick as if he was the dumbest creature ever to slither the crusty earth. And while the quiet man's intellect may not have appeared to be much more than average, that was actually the one aspect of Erick Strickt that was not at all as it appeared....

✿

At the Budheuser Beer merchandise distribution warehouse (near the interstate highway and situated between Shemwell's Pharmaceuticals distribution center and the new mayonnaise factory), Erick Strickt was the Tap Marker Dept. for the entire Middle West.

If a barkeep in Milwaukee, Wisconsin, required a Budheuser tap marker (that is, the decorative knob on which one pulls to draw beer from its respective tap), it was Erick Strickt of Hubbard, Illinois, who took the order, found the item in his immense inventory (roughly 200 of each of 53 different decorative knobs – 10,600 knobs boxed five-to-a-box and stacked ceiling high along the western wall of his windowless-but-fluorescent concrete workroom), and dispatched the item expeditiously.

If a bar and grill in Akron, Ohio, required an O'Hanlon's tap marker (O'Hanlon's being the Budheuser response to trendy, darker Irish imports), it was from Erick Strickt that it was sent and received.

And whenever a neighborhood tavern in Detroit, Michigan, required a replacement for a broken Python tap marker (Python, a malt, being another spin-off of the Budheuser machine), it was the thoroughly average Erick Strickt of Hubbard, Illinois, who sent it.

Thus, over thirty-plus years of employment, Erick Strickt (who did not consume alcohol) became probably the most famous, unseen costar in the liquor-fueled dramas that unfolded nightly in dimly lit mead houses across the Old Northwest.

Thirty-plus years (bless his heart): "Hey, Strickt – wasn't you workin' for these guys back when they's still 'cross town? In the ol' biscuit fact'ry?" asked a much younger co-worker at Erick's thirtieth anniversary reception (in the break room, featuring a Dairy Barn ice cream cake cut into tiny squares and a cooler full of lemonade; Erick received a sarcastic greeting card about being old and unmarried, and a gold-plated bookmark that brandished an extra-long tassel and had the words *ENOUGH ALREADY!* engraved on it).

Erick smiled broadly. "Yessir. But back then the joint weren't owned by Budheuser itself. We's a contracted, independent warehouse – R&M Advertising, owned by the late Mr. Bill Rexing."

And Jacob Shiner laughed loudly: "Biggest tight ass this town ever seen."

And the room laughed, too, but Erick Strickt, in a rare display of spine, asserted his strong disagreement, jumping to his feet to address the casual assembly, projecting his quiet baritone as no one had expected as he spoke in defense of the dead: "Mr. Bill Rexing hired me at min'mum wage thirty years ago when my leg was still in a cast..."

"Howdja break it?" Rodney Hobbs called out, interrupting with genuine curiosity (his fatal flaw in most conversations).

Erick ignored him. "And no matter what the econ'my was like, and you remember how much it sucked in the '80s, Bill Rexing's men always got some sorta annual raise, and weren't none of us ever laid off

every other equally average man to whom Erick had worked in close proximity over the last thirty years...completely average individuals (just like him) who had contributed to the residue of dissatisfaction that clung to the warehouse walls like cigar smoke...thoroughly negative energy that survived its cultivators (at best, the typical warehouse employee lasted only one-tenth the duration of Erick Strickt's tenure), but which found perpetuation in the mantras embraced by three decades of "peers."

This job sucks.

I don't git paid near what I'm worth.

If I could afford it, I'd walk right outta here 'n git me a better job.

But no one ever walked – the short tenures of Erick's co-workers were almost always the result of stupid mistakes made by the workers themselves...a number of times...so they were inevitably turned loose: Mark Seats – late to work six times in one month with no better reason than "jus' movin' a l'il slow this mornin'"; Pat Tyrell – failed a mandatory drug test after having crashed a forklift into an extra row of holiday beer steins (such accidents were common in November and December as product piled up for Christmas orders...but that didn't explain the THC in the bald man's pubic hair); Randall "Randy" Mitchell – asked a female employee out on a date and failed to accept her negative response...seventeen times; Trish Alstadt – asked another female employee out on a date and failed to accept her negative response...thirteen times....

It took him weeks to make the connection, but he finally made it: These were the same men (and women), two hundred years later, working at half-productivity for higher wages, and doing so because….

"Job security," Jacob Shiner had explained with a sly smile when he confronted Erick about the latter's quip in the break room and Erick responded by describing his frustration with the epiphany he'd experienced. "Ya make a job take twice as long so that there's always a reason to come back tomorrow." (With a sly smile.)

And the perfectly average Erick Strickt, for the first time in his unremarkable life, knew a knowing he had never known, and just as he owed his lifelong employment to Jacob Shiner, he now likewise owed this latest recognition of previously unrecognized cognition to the same Jacob Shiner, whose contempt for "authority" (and not any specific authority, mind you, just authority in general) sent Erick's brain heaving….

And a heaving brain makes no sound.

Thus did Erick Strickt greet Jacob Shiner's deceptive work ethic with three years of silence.

So: On the same day Andrew Shiner drank lemon-fresh ammonia and choked on steel wool, Erick Strickt found himself in the same break room wherein he had been fêted for having kept the same job for thirty years, found himself squished between Jacob Shiner and Stacy Hilt (who was the only female on the loading dock), and found himself being told that by the end of the year his job at the warehouse would join the dodo and the carrier pigeon on the extinction list.

In fact, everyone in the tiny break room (112 mostly average, adult human beings) were suddenly squished and (in six months) unemployed.

Jacob Shiner rolled his eyes, cursed quietly under his breath.

Stacy Hilt began to cry, cursing softly under her breath.

Soon, the entire room was quickly awash with sighing and crying and quiet cursing...except for Erick Strickt, who (instantly disgusted) stood up and began to winnow his way to the exit (though he hadn't been dismissed).

The Suit at the front of the room turned to a nearby worker and quizzed him regarding Erick's name before addressing him: "You've not been dismissed, Mr. Strickt."

And 111 heads swiveled to regard the quiet man, who had stopped and turned to smile at the Middle Management Representative, who didn't smile back.

Erick opened his mouth in an exaggerated suggestion that he might speak, but...

...but the Corporate Gerent at the front of the room was suddenly two hundred years old and identical (*identical!*) to the men who had run the salt works, closing one operation to make more money at another operation, just as when the original salt industry in Illinois shut down in 1873. Hundreds of coal miners and lumberjacks and salt workers were left unemployed because it was cheaper to mine salt with machinery elsewhere.

Suddenly, the Soft-Handed Administrator was just another Uneasy Over-Compensator chasing profits wherever it led him, and the truth was that a distribution center in Texas could move more product more quickly with a rotating crew of sixty poorly paid migrant workers than at the Hubbard warehouse.

And so Erick Strickt, who read at a fourth grade level (but who had purchased a single share of Budheuser stock every year he worked there, and which the Franks had bought from him for $500 each), smiled at the squished and the saddened as he silently turned and walked out, his disappointment held at bay by the strange triumph he felt after all these years...connections made and realizations manifested...nothing ever changes...and knowing so makes survival much, much easier....

In the registry, however, the citizens boarded at the Poor Farm were classified (in Homer's careful script) according to their respective circumstances/situations upon their arrival:

Pleasant Haskins – aged 59 yrs., 4 ms., 22ds. - 12th December 1925 -
Incapable/Impoverished.

Alice Clark – aged 55yrs., 8 ms., 13 ds. - 19th July 1926 -
Defective.

Jane Spitsinger – aged 67yrs., 6ms., 7ds. - 23rd March 1927 -
Widow/Impoverished/Pneumonia.

"Incapable" signified some form of handicap that made it impossible for one to live alone. Pleasant Haskins, for instance, was an epileptic.

"Defective" signified some form of developmental delay. Alice Clark, for example, had Down's Syndrome.

Classifications were listed in the order of their perceived significance, which meant that in the eyes of the County Poor Farm (that is, Homer Henduck), Jane Spitsinger's greatest reason for her social redundancy was that she had no man.

As Mistress of the Manor, Marion Henduck also functioned *in loco parentis*, mothering her adult orphans as many had likely never experienced...and not a single step of her duties did she bemoan or shirk – particularly regarding the widow Spitsinger, with whom Marion had been in a number of civic organizations: the Hubbard Ladies Auxiliary; the Hubbard Belles (a womens' chorus); the Hubbard Quilters' Guild;

The Hubbard Literary Circle; and the Hubbard Temperance Society (an anti-liquor organization from which Marian had resigned in 1922 when the society quietly accepted a hundred dollar donation from the Ku Kux Klan earmarked for the cultivation of temperance amongst the darker-skinned members of the community).

The poor widow Spitsinger, whom Marian Henduck loved: Despite the compassionate embrace with which she greeted her duties, when the former arrived on the latter's doorstep with suitcases and a chesty cough, the other fifty-two residents at the Farm suddenly became a little less relevant even to their community of last resort.

Things changed and did so drastically. Fresh water was no longer delivered to bedroom wash basins every morning – the incapable now fetched their own. The daily collection of laundry was no longer an opportunity for Marian to chat with her wards – soiled linens and clothing were now to be quietly deposited into a large wicker basket at the bottom of the main staircase. Likewise, dinner was no longer an immense, group affair involving three rooms of adult orphans gathered around tables, standing in corners, squished onto sofas, and all visiting between bites, like the chatter heard in any busy lunch room. Instead, meals were now buffet affairs and residents were encouraged to come and go at their leisure, but to do so quickly...and quietly.

Indeed, in late March, 1927, Marian Henduck enjoyed a terrific metamorphosis as she suddenly focused the best of her abilities and the majority of her concern onto Jane Spitsinger, whose chest heaved with phlegm as she lay drowning in her own room, which was arranged in a corner of the third floor of the farmhouse (the old attic, which Homer had renovated and finished to create an expansive dormitory for ladies with a smaller, single room for extreme and/or seriously contagious cases like Jane...except that when Jane arrived there were already three women in residence with varying stages of pneumonia, and two more presenting early manifestations of consumption.

So how did the impoverished widow score the single room?

Marian Henduck *loved* Jane Spitsinger.

And so it was that on the eighteenth day of April, in the Year of Our Lord nineteen hundred and twenty-seven, and of the Independence of these United States of America one hundred and fifty-one, Homer Henduck (who was born *Theophilus* Henduck, but dubbed "Homer" by his older, lisping brother) turned out his bedside lamp, crawled beneath the covers of the vast bed he shared with Marian (the mattress, springs, and iron frame as old as their vows) and assumed his usual, coffin-ready position – flat on his back, legs crossed at the ankles, hands folded atop his modest gut, his daytime It-Could-Always-Be-Worse smile having diminished to a cozy, sleepy-time grin. His bride, whom he had always known (though they lived a township apart, the Henducks and the Cornockers had come to the county together in 1851, having initially met as fellow laborers at the salt works a decade earlier; for over seventy years the families had become increasingly woven into each others lives through friendship, society, worship, and DNA – both he and his lisping older brother, Seamus [that is, Jim], had married Cornocker women, who had proven to be hearty, reasonable, fertile helpmates over the last forty years)...Homer's bride lay slightly propped on her right elbow, her back to her husband, her lamp burning low, and a Campbellite commentary spread open beside her.

She rolled her eyes. Homer crawled and settled, and the bed bounced and shook, creaked and cracked, and she rolled her eyes....

She furrowed her brow. Homer breathed his heavy Another-Day-Done sigh, and she furrowed her brow....

She cried. Her husband mumbled something from behind closed eyes...before his breath gave way to a gentle snore...and she cried....

"You are sorely missed," he had said.

And, *ohhh*, she cried so gently that neither sound nor movement was detected (indeed, just as she had learned to do in the course of her life amongst men), her eyes full of tears, but not to the point of spillage, her throat tight with feelings, but stifled by clenched jaws.

For three weeks now she had been so absorbed in her perceived duties to the widow that she had never once considered being missed, nor had she ever imagined that the sense of family she had worked so hard to cultivate amongst the Poor Farm community had actually taken root.

God, she missed her children. Fiercely. Missed feeling needed, feeling loved...and Homer had always been as good as useless for such needs, except on Wednesday nights when beers with a select crew of Poor Farm men would unleash the repressed pubescent inside of him and he would avail himself of his marital privilege (sometimes for as long as twelve minutes), then pass out.

So she embraced her duties to the orphans and loved them, but had never stopped to imagine that she was loved in return.

Rather, she had sought redemption in the simple virtue of her own busy compassion.

The arrival of Jane, however, had complicated everything.

What She Read: Every night, the Campbellite commentary lay open beside her, and every night she read the same passage, lifted straight from the King James and bracketed by the Nineteenth Century understanding of the commentary author (Dr. P.A. Gortimer Saggs, whose doctorate was the rough equivalent of declaring oneself a plow because one had spent three years sleeping in a barn).

Every night, this is what she read:

Who can find a virtuous woman? For her price is far above rubies.
The heart of her husband doth safely trust in her
so that he shall have no need of spoil.
She will do him good and not evil all the days of her life.

Et cetera….

Redemption: From May, 1918 through November, 1924, the widow Jane Spitsinger and the farmer's bride, Marian Henduck, were engaged in such a potentially scandalous arrangement of intimacy that even the present author (a century on) hesitates to describe it.

But...if you must know: Weekly, having traveled together into town for worship, the ladies would take lunch a block away at Colly's Dining Room, the echo of that morning's sermon still fresh in their ears, the pair still humming the dismissal hymn...and there they would remain, chattering away as waves of Methodists flowed in and out, then Baptists, and the four-square building in which Colly's was situated heaved with hungry Messianics, their blessings counted, their judgments affirmed, their faces a-glow in fellowship, their souls washed in the cleansing Blood of the Lamb and oblivious to the Campbellite women seated in the southwest corner, near the exit to the ice shed, smiling sweetly, their voices low, their hands linked beneath the table cloth – the widow Spitsinger (who did her husband good all the days of his life) and Marian Henduck (in whom her husband's heart did safely trust)....

And should your salivating curiosity require further satisfaction, know this: In Jane Spitsinger's pony cart, it took approximately thirty minutes to travel from the County Poor Farm (situated on the low ridge east of town, and a half-mile south of the Spitsinger farm) to the Campbellite church in town (and vice versa)...except on Sundays when, regardless of weather, the return trip took *hours....*

So: When the dying Jane Spitsinger arrived on the Poor Farm porch, it had been roughly two-and-a-half years since the ladies had ridden to worship together, the widow having discovered and pursued the thoroughly appropriate companionship of the widower Daniel Slack, who was ten years her junior and taught twelve children of varying ages at the Ellis Township schoolhouse, his wife having perished a year before Jane's husband and previously kept isolated by his grief and responsibility to the school.

Marian, meanwhile, had begun walking to worship at the Sugar Camp Primitive Baptist Church, a quarter of a mile south of the Poor Farm.

So by the time the former arrived on the latter's doorstep, Marian had spent roughly two-and-a-half years thoroughly devoted to her adult orphans, her heart jaggedly mended after the abrupt ending of her companionship with the widow...two-and-a-half years of unswerving service, dedication, and distraction...through which she felt redeemed...but hardly virtuous.

Virtuous: The agriculturalist's spouse loved Jane Spitsinger, and the guilty scar that scissored its way across her conscience ripped clean open when she spotted the bedraggled remnant of her Sunday Friend slouching into the farmhouse foyer, a bent cardboard valise in each hand, a roaring wet cough building in her chest and throat.

From the shadowed landing of the main staircase Marian had silently watched her husband receive her former lover, watched him register her in the big book beneath the telephone, then watched them approach the staircase....

The companionship of the bookish Danny Slack had fizzled quickly as the old school in which he taught was absorbed into the Hubbard Municipal School District...at his exclusion...so he had turned his attention to improving and selling the eighty acres he owned northeast of the Spitsinger farm...at Jane's exclusion...and now here she was, her existence reduced to two flimsy suitcases, her clothes turned dingy, her hair now tangled and so, so gray....

How fragile the widow now appeared – gaunt, hungry, lonely...and how...how did Marian Henduck feel, watching the widow arrive?

She felt discovered, worried, heartbroken.... Naturally, Homer had never once considered or suspected his bride of anything outside of the template his own mother had provided as he grew up (which was, of course, one of perfection), but on the darkened landing of the main staircase Marian felt thoroughly exposed, her most private wishes and dreams (unknown even to Homer)...her most private wishes and dreams now took wing (she imagined), bursting from her chest and out of the top of her own graying head, leaving her empty and small, the persona she had cultivated now burning in a heap around her booted feet (or so she imagined)....

The widow Spitsinger.

Jane.

Urgently, Marian raced to the attic floor in advance of Homer and their new ward (who was moving very slowly, indeed) and began tidying the single room, stripping the tiny bed of its sheets, gingerly flipping the mattress, re-dressing the bed, emptying the trash, banging, clanging....

Virginia Pearson (*47 yrs., 8ms., 18ds.; Spinster/Impoverished/ Pneumonia*) heard the racket, rose from her bed (where she had been nursing an abridged version of *The Count of Monte Cristo*), and shuffled across the splintery wooden floor to investigate.

"New arrival?" (*Cough, cough.*)

But no answer wafted back to her from the blur of arms and sheets that was Marian Henduck.

(*Cough, cough.*) "New arrival?"

And still no answer as Virginia now shuffled into the doorway, heaved a deeper cough, then repeated her query.

"New arrival?"

And Marian stopped abruptly, swiveled on her heels to glare at the diminutive Virginia (five feet tall at her best, ninety-five pounds at her healthiest, mousy always, but capable of producing a wet trumpet of a cough unrivaled by any of her also-dying peers), and though she opened her mouth to speak, Marian only cried, openly but silently sobbing before sweeping the drowning spinster off her feet in a brilliant, engulfing embrace.

"Um," said Virginia when Marian sniffled in her ear.

"Gah esh goo," the superintendent's wife now sniffle-cried into Virginia's bony shoulder, which was growing moist.

"Ma'am?"

And Marian straightened, sniffled, wiped her eyes, and smiled broadly, even issuing a wispy chuckle.

"God is good, Virginia," she repeated, retrieving a handkerchief from her apron pocket. "After all my doubt and selfishness...after all the love I've wasted, lost, hidden, He continues to offer me redemption through good works!"

And skinny Ginny coughed as she brightened and choked on the Word of God: "Faith without works (*cough, cough*) is dead (*hack, wheeze*)."

The women embraced again.

"Indeed!" yelped Marian as she gazed past Virginia's shoulder to see the figure emerging in the third floor doorway...the dying widow Spitsinger....

✿

Jane Spitsinger was horrified by her final situation.

Particularly, she was horrified by a lifetime of bad decision-making, which had dramatically pulled her out of one of the most prominent local families (that being the family of Dr. Dye, whose mineral springs resort had brought brief notoriety to town) and delivered her to a lifetime of agriculture and homemaking...neither of which she felt was beneath her, but which she either didn't understand or enjoy.

She had met Joe Spitsinger at church – a moderately handsome young man who worked the family farm, was brawny in the best of ways, funny, literate (steeped in Scripture), and seemingly civilized in a way undiscovered by his male peers.

That is, he played the violin.

Not the fiddle – the violin, and there were nights during their brief courtship (four weeks) when he would play the sweetest, saddest hymns he could conjure and she would damn near swoon.

Thus were the sixteen year old Jane and twenty year old Joe quickly engaged, swiftly married, and four boys were sired in five years...but the violin disappeared soon after the eager vows were uttered, and literacy slowly gave way to coarseness, and humor was increasingly and inexplicably replaced by anger...a great deal of anger that often found expression in violence – towards her, the boys, the animals (once, in a fit of anger that had seemingly begun with Jane's weak coffee at breakfast and grew to include tirades about the dry summer, the cost of hay, and the suspicious sideways glances he perceived from the goats, Joe snapped the necks of two kids who had slipped out of the goat house and were wandering toward the pond)....

Worse still, Jane Spitsinger (née Dye) had been irrevocably and unilaterally disowned by her family as soon as she had announced her engagement to the common farmer, Joe. The portrait of pretense and Yankee aristocracy, her father, Dr. Isaiah William Dye, was to the health profession what George Hearst was to gold speculation, emerging from the east coast to mine the local settlers of the lucre they would freely spend for seemingly sound medical attention. When he discovered three other like-minded physicians already in practice in Hubbard, however, he correctly judged the leanings of the community and turned to quackery – Dr. Dye's Healing Mineral Springs, which made available the healing properties of the briny springs that lay just below the sod in the rear quarter of the doctor's land. For just pennies an hour, the puny settler could rest his weary bones (up to the chest) in a shallow hole brimming with "Nature's Medicine" for as long as he wished, provided he engaged in no lewd or unclean act(s). For sure, the doctor was quite eager to offer "scientific" medical advice for considerably more money, but from May through September the springs were what paid for the mansion.

The Mansion: From the bird's-eye perch of the third floor study of his brick, hilltop home, the doctor sat above it all, like a Thegn surveying his tenants, largely untouched by the population he defrauded (minus the requisite smiling and mingling at church).

And his lack of positive regard for the mostly-Southerner community grew no better the longer he stayed.

In fact, Jane had once recalled to Marion how her father had systematically presented her and each of her siblings (including Jane, seven girls and one boy, all schooled at home with varying success by a Massachusetts school marm the doctor had imported once the boy, Isaiah, Jr., was school age) with the same ultimatum: if they could not, in their lifetimes, attract the attentions of well-bred Easterners, they were never to marry at all, lest they voluntarily forsake their family and inheritance.

Thus are there six spinsters and one bachelor named Dye planted side-by-side with their father and mother near the front of the old cemetery by the reservoir.

Jane Spitsinger lies somewhere beneath runway #5 of the Hubbard Municipal Airport.

Mind you, none of the above is meant to suggest that Jane's married life would have been much different (if at all) had she lured some well-bred Easterner – in her eyes, the apparent gap between an educated shyster (as she felt her father had become) and a quick-to-anger dirt worshipper (as her father had named the local farming population, employing a pejorative label typically reserved for the "savage" Native) was paltry...except her father victimized thousands of people a year; Joe Spitsinger "only" ever abused and degraded his own household....

✿

And now here she was – dwindling rapidly in a rented bed at the County Poor Farm, her deepest regret hovering at her bedside, carrying on with gossip, reading to her...without any solicitation and without either of them mentioning the obvious past, Marian Henduck had instantly dedicated herself to the constant care of Jane Spitsinger and dutifully closeted herself daily with her special, reluctant ward....

"Perhaps you would help me walk the floor?" Jane wondered aloud one afternoon soon after she took refuge at the farm, interrupting Marian's awkward reading of the prophet Amos.

Marian smiled...condescendingly. "No, no," she purred, "rest is the best medicine for you."

"But I can't help imagining that just a turn around the floor might...invigorate me...even just a little."

And Marian expanded the same damn smile. "I have it on very good advice – "

"Please, Marian – "

"Very sound advice delivered as my own mother lay suff'rin from yer very same cough – "

"Silly advice that killed your mother."

"Not at all. Mother was old – "

"So am I!" (*Cough, wheeze, cough.*) "Please, Marian – "

"Twas yer own father who declared bed rest the best curative – yer own father who now speaks to ya from the past and tells ya that the *only* way to dry up yer lungs is ta *lay still 'n don't move a muscle.* I will treat yer needs."

Sighing slightly: "Oh, Marian...."

"Are ya thirsty?"

"No."

"Warm?"

"Yes."

"But comftr'ble?"

"Yes."

"Shall I continya in *Amos* or wouldja perfer the newspaper?"

And so on....

And Jane was horrified – torpedoed from beyond the grave by her father...one final shot designed to sink her...completely....

Meanwhile, Marian was sorely missed....

When Jane Spitsinger was buried on the third day of May, 1927, it was the first day in a fortnight since the sun had dared show its face.

Since its arrival in late March, Spring had proven to be nothing it ever promised to be and rebirth was taking its time as the gray of Winter lingered like a drunken guest, casting its dripping shadow over the entire, muddy landscape, the trees budding only modestly, the Easter Lilies having never even bloomed, the tulips still barely ascendant....

And into the sunlight emerged the skinny, pale corpse of the widow Jane, her slim and flimsy casket open (Marian had asked that the sun be allowed to shine on the body as it was conveyed) and carefully balanced in the hands of her anonymous Poor Farm counterparts who carried her from the front porch, across the lawn, and down the hill to the small cemetery where Homer stood, shovel in hand, squinting in the morning light....

Rising at four that morning to the urging of a third floor resident who insisted she check on the widow, Marian had barely even absorbed the passing before she was sending Homer to call the doctor, fetch the paperwork, and dig a grave. Within ninety minutes of waking, then, she was busily (and with surprising stoicism) washing the remains, which she dressed in Jane's best Sunday dress, then disappeared to make breakfast, after which the men would gather to deliver the latest of their number to the paupers' field, where dozens of small wooden crosses leaned toward the east....

But now hush and stand with them and watch....

Stand with the silent survivors as Homer, without speaking, shatters the morning, hammering the lid onto the coffin (every thud echoing to the kitchen, where Marian...)....

Watch as the men move in quiet precision, straining to gracefully lower the box into the shallow grave (four feet, which made remains easily retrieved should family-come-lately wish them exhumed). Earlier, from this spot, Homer had paused to watch the first visible sunrise in fourteen days and had felt momentarily ashamed for smiling....

They reach for their shovels...they bury their dead....

Stand here, hat in your hand, and feel your planet spinning and groaning as the action generates the passage of time....

X. "In Yer Face, Fred Flintstone!"

My son is playing with dinosaurs.

For Christmas,
he received
twenty-five
miniature dinosaurs
of varying sizes,
all made of solid plastic,
which is derived from oil,
which is 100%
dinosaur resin.

My son is playing with dinosaurs.

until some twenty-odd stones were face down in the springtime mud...no reason for it, just a late night skirmish (a romp, really), born of boredom and which wasn't initially meant to involve knocking anything over (a mere slalom through a row of the cheapest, most easily defiled graves in the burial ground)....

As punishment, Ron's friend spent that summer mowing grass at the cemetery, while Ron spent it helping out around the funeral parlor...including yard work and plenty of heavy lifting and carrying anything from tables, chairs, and desks to caskets, casket stands, and pianos...and having once napped in one of the newer, state-of-the-art caskets kept in the basement showroom (when he should have been trimming a hedge), he was now further amused by the memory of how, standing near the casket at his great uncle Harold's wake, he had noticed that the family had arranged for his grandfather's brother to be buried in a Tranquil Repose casket and was heard to mumble to the departed, "Oh, you lucky thing...".

Not that the man standing at the bay window in his dining room, clothed only in his flannel bathrobe and nursing a cold cup of yesterday's coffee was counting down the days to his own dirt nap, but any longtime insomniac is doomed to drool slightly at the apparent coziness of anything bed-like.

Even this particular morning had come on the heels of a sleepless night full of pointless hope. He had pursued sleep in 45 minute intervals, rewarding his concentration with an occasional cigarette (which probably didn't help), rising to adjourn to the living room, lighting the tobacco with a gold-plated lighter another friend had given him for being Best Man in his wedding...which Ron had also managed to screw up....

Lately, without expectation or warning, he had begun to recognize the smell of citrus (just a hint) and could find himself looking around for a source, would fail to find it, would miss it when it was gone....

Mid-morning at work, he recognized the scent and his nose twitched as he looked up and scanned the classroom...26 strangely silent teenagers sitting as if in prayer, their heads bowed as they engaged with Atticus Finch...and they all smelled, just not of citrus...

...and then it was gone.

Without thinking, he allowed himself to be seen sniffing the air and the student assistant couldn't resist: "Smell somethin'?" she asked in nothing resembling a whisper.

A buoyant personality, the assistant. Privately horrified by her own girth, she was a classic over-compensator, distracting her unsuspecting peers with humor, sass, and cloth ears (re: her speaking volume – never, since the invention of the microphone, had so many simple, declarative sentences been spoken as loudly as they had since this child, now a high school senior, learned to talk).

I'm right here, he thought, *why are you yelling?*

"I thought I did, yes," he nodded, then smiled as a giggle skittered its way toward him from the far corner of the room.

"That was me," a tiny boy yodeled/giggled, likewise over-compensating for being diminutive by encouraging others to laugh at him, and while a handful of students vaguely attempted to stifle their own laughter, the rest roared on cue and suddenly Harper Lee's manuscript was abandoned in deference to the tiny boy's fart (which was, indeed, lurid and green)...all traces of citrus now gone....

"Return to your reading, please," he urged, the entire class now a-titter over flatulence.

"What'd *you* think it was?" the assistant barked, her face spreading in a sarcastic smile.

"I dunno," he shrugged and returned his gaze to the class roster, which he had spent the last twenty minutes checking and re-checking...all present...all accounted for....

He didn't eat at lunchtime. Never did. In fact, breakfast and lunch were always of identical substance.

These days, sometimes supper was, too.

Coffee and cigarettes.

At lunch, the cigarette was queen, enjoyed hurriedly as he drove the limits of what he referred to as "Old Town" – that part of the community that dated back to the days preceding 1888, when a freak February tornado razed much of the town and killed over thirty citizens. Stop signs included, it was a twenty minute circuit; just long enough to smoke the cigarettes he'd been craving for the last three hours, stop at the gas station on the east side of town for a fresh, tall polystyrene cup of Special Blend coffee, then smoke another cigarette before returning to work.

Every day, 11.45 to 12.05, a cigarette clasped in a two-fingered, left handed pinch and awake with evil, he drove his circle around the center of town, departing the Casey Avenue parking lot and heading south on Seventh Street to Newby, then west on Newby, passing the derelict shopping center....

But, wait: Making the sharp, right-hand turn onto Newby, the breeze through the open window seemed to translate the sprawling tobacco plume into wafting citrus, and as he slowed to a crawl he felt it shift so as to completely fill his flaring nostrils....

Although an imagined sensation, he had begun to think of the occurrence of citrus as signifying *presence* (which his subconscious had likely anticipated when it conjured the sense memories of her hand lotion, her shampoo, her lip gloss on Christmas Day as they stood outside her aunt's house, shivering and smoking, huddling closer and closer...), so when he sniffed the air it was in deep, almost desperate gasps that made him appear to be drowning.

Expanding his chest, he tossed the cigarette out through the window in an attempt to isolate the scent, and once the smoke had gone he expanded his chest again in a long inhalation that anticipated the realization of *presence*...but was only air....

Hey: About that wedding he screwed up...it couldn't have otherwise been more beautiful. Held on the patio atop the Budheuser Law Building at the university where the nuptializing duo had met and dated, Ron had just finished admiring the entire scene as it played it out just in front of him – his handsome friends practically shimmering in the May sunshine as they exchanged a lifetimes worth of vows – when he felt the potato salad from lunch move in the pit of his stomach, which emitted a squirting noise, and his tuxedo suddenly seemed to tighten as his forehead became moist with sweat. The minister asked the crowd of witnesses if any felt compelled to dissent, and the Best Man felt his knees become elastic, unreliable, his stomach a swashbuckling mess of nerves, heat, and spoiled mayonnaise...then the ring....

The ring! For some strange reason echoing a child's attachment to his favorite toy or blanket, Ron had loaded his tuxedo pockets with every ordinary item he could fit – his keys, the golden lighter, a full pack of Camels, half a pack of cinnamon gum, his wallet, a mechanical pencil, a crumpled handkerchief, sixty-eight cents in dimes and pennies, and the ring. Finally fishing it free of a pocket, the ring found further freedom slipping through Ron's jittery, sweaty fingers and onto the tiled patio floor, where it rolled into a crack behind the plastic potted plant to the right of Ron's shaking legs.

See it now: He bends to pick up the ring and the minister (a Baptist pastor) leads the witnesses in a nervous group chuckle ("Technical difficulties," is his pithy prompt to the hundred or so uncomfortable friends and family who have long since already rolled their eyes and shaken their heads at Ron's ruination of the event at hand). He rises quickly, ring in hand, and the witnesses politely chuckle (a smattering even applaud) as he hands the ring to the stoic groom (who had, only seconds earlier, been so moved by the present rites that he had twice choked with tears as he spoke his vows, but who was now suddenly cold and disapproving, his eye contact firm and scolding). The Best Man now laughs a quiet, but goofy and staccato laugh that has remained largely dormant since the third grade and booger jokes, but which now seems to reveal to God and everyone (or, at least, Pastor Jeff and the assembled guests) just who, exactly, Ron Colly is....

Or was....

Disappointed, he pulled into the parking lot of the old shopping center, rumbling to a stop as he crossed the railroad tracks that striped the asphalt plateau. The old railroad car shops that had previously been the savior of the community (now sixty years gone) once occupied this land and, perhaps as a nod to that industrial legacy, the tracks had always been left partially exposed, regardless of the various modest attempts to revitalize the property. Even with the Post Office recently relocating to the site, the tracks had been spared in the patched lot.

The Post Office, a Family Dollar store, and an IGA were now all that occupied the otherwise decrepit space – a perfume of mold covering the expanses between stores, the empty store fronts presenting a muddled face of mixed media: glass, metal, rust, wood, and bad grammar.

Amanda Back Bitches!, read the spray-painted warning alongside the south wall of the old Montgomery Ward's store.

It grieved him, the tragic death of apostrophe-s at the hands of popular culture, rising from the State-sponsored half-literacy of an impoverished minority to receive adoption in the widespread mainstream popular culture embraced by even completely literate, wealthier communities.

Populism (which typically only nurtured fear and paranoia) at its best.

Indeed, 'twas the story of the English language itself.

Too bad it sounded so damn stupid.

❀

Amanda Back Bitches!

He had written the phrase on the chalkboard at work and asked, "What's wrong with this sentence?"

Again, the class dissolved into a circular ripple of laughter before a boy seated halfway up the middle row (where there was no laughter) suggested placing a comma after *Back*. Meanwhile, the clearly unhappy (and certainly not laughing) girl seated next to him proudly engaged in a confession of guilt by association, Amanda being not just *a* friend, but her *best* friend.

"Is Amanda's last name *Back*?" he asked.

"No," she snapped, her head a-swivel, lips increasingly terse, and her thin skin a-bristle with the urge to take offense on behalf of her vandal friend.

A beat, then he silently placed an apostrophe-s after *Amanda* before explaining that when a word is combined with the present tense, singular conjugation of the verb *to be* (is), an apostrophe-s is appropriate.

Silence.

"I thought it showed ownership," she shot back, surprising him with the possibility that she may have, at some point, paid attention….

❧

Ownership: A block past the echoing shopping center, on the southwest and northwest corners of Newby and Tenth streets were the hollow structures that had once housed a paint store and a grocery, respectively. To Ron, however, the significance of both structures was that ninety-odd years earlier, the former had housed his great grandfather's restaurant while the latter had been the site of Great Grandpa's furniture store (though the current empty building was of newer construction). Both were ruined and lost in the Great Depression (his ancestor's own heart also ultimately failing in 1937, aged 56), and his family had endured a long, slow recovery in the generations since….

Daily, driving past this corner, he had imagined its appearance before the bottom fell out, trying to conjure an extrapolated image in his mind based on the yellow photograph he'd preserved at home – his great grandfather, Joseph, sitting on a crate in front of the restaurant bearing his name, his legs stretched out and propped up on the truck of a young tree (now also gone), his ankles crossed. Another man (whose name is lost, but whose funny moustache is the classic, curled, handlebar style common to silent movie villains) is seated on a crate opposite him, offering only his profile, and neither are smiling (indeed, when remembering the photograph, Ron had often wondered about the nature of the culture shift that separated the stoic gazes of most Nineteenth and early Twentieth century photographs from the current photographic obligation to smile one's ass off…). Joseph is clean-shaven, thin, of modest stature (as is Ron); the other appears taller, thicker. The restaurant behind them is thriving.

Thriving: Previously he had been content to drive past this spot and let his imagination peel back the losses as he continued on, but today, having pulled over, he finally decided to insert himself into the scene, to position himself in the exact spot where his great grandfather (forty years gone by the time Ron was born) once posed for a photograph…to reach out in the darkness of a lunchtime daydream in the hopes of identifying more of himself that he had otherwise failed to recognize….

Hey: About those graves he vandalized twenty years ago…he's sorry, you know…has been since he did it….

They were among the oldest graves in the entire three-acre cemetery, which began as a small, country cemetery not long after the establishment of the community itself. Originally, the graves had been intentionally separated from the other older graves at the front of the burial ground, but as the community grew so did the graveyard become increasingly swollen until newer graves began to fill the divide. Further, a July storm a few years earlier had claimed a number of the big, old trees that had originally defined and separated the graves in front (the town's first mayor, several doctors, a robber baron of the local railroad, some politicians) from those in the back. The shade was now more sparse as one moved among the stones, the tree stumps lining each pathway at irregular intervals like hitching posts for the phantom horses of the Apocalypse. More than ever before, the gap between the prominent at the front and the unknown at the back was now subject to visible bridging....

Hey: Those graves Ron accidentally vandalized twenty years ago were vulnerable only because they were hidden – the graves of Hubbard's poorest citizens, mostly black, their names poorly etched into lumpy, cement headstones and smeared by weather, some already cracked, just itchin' to crumble, just askin' for a quick and heavy hand to send 'em topplin'...no signs of visitors outside of some tracks left by a riding mower....

Oh, and hey: The judge who had given Ron and his accomplice the chance to work off their crimes through volunteerism was also a longstanding member of the local airport authority, which acted on behalf of the county regarding the operation of a small airport east of town.

In fact, the judge had chaired the committee tasked with identifying a location for said airport (the former site of the County Poor Farm) and, several months later, it was under the watchful eyes of the same judge that workers began re-locating the hundred-plus graves cradled in the Poor Farm cemetery to the back of the old cemetery by the reservoir.

But the process was laborious, time consuming, and expensive, about all of which the County Board complained (and the judge concurred), so construction began with only a quarter of the graves moved.

Thus does Jane Spitsinger (née Dye) lay somewhere beneath Runway #5 of the Hubbard Municipal Airport.

✿

He walked to the corner where the old paint store was...where the restaurant was...and waited for the arrival of noon, sensing the tiniest shift of shadows as the sun reached the summit of its local journey.

Turning to face the intersection, he imagined it as it may have been before the bottom fell out...the car shops and their constant repair and production of the locomotive, their production yard surrounded and half-hidden by fencing, only the tops of the locomotives visible from the street and the inner workings of the yard known only by the soundings of the siren – a signal at the start of the day, at lunch, and to end the day...the economic spine of the community a-throb and strong, and....

Amanda Back Bitches! The bright red declaration of return was also a-throb, pulsating on the wall of the shopping center like neon signage, a gauntlet thrown down at the semi-literate feet of anyone who might dare take umbrage at the message or the girl herself.

Amanda Back Bitches! Regardless of one's acquaintance with the girl, or whether anyone had even noticed she was gone in the first place, everyone now knew that she was back and armed with spray paint.

"Apostrophe-s does, indeed, show ownership," he had confirmed for the student at work, smiling the rehearsed smile of positive reinforcement, "but it also serves a second function when a word is combined with *is*."

And in the silence that followed, as he awaited a sign of either understanding or concession, he felt it...and he felt it now, standing on the corner of Tenth and Newby, the car shops gone for two generations, the shopping center bereft...he felt it – a humidity of failure as potent and as tangible as the moldy musk hovering around the darkened, broken store fronts and as heavy on his straining heart as teaching grammar to high school sophomores is intellectually dismaying.

The cameras at work are watching, and they record *everything* "just in case"...but they don't see the man crumble internally when he teaches the language and a painted teenager in a flimsy, pink tank top (the word *Princess* silk-screened in sparkly letters across her padded chest) looks him in the eye, swivels her sassy head and says, "So?"

So: *Amanda Back Bitches!* And she ain't brought nuttin' wid 'er 'cept hard feelins and a whole lotta spare time – a clear asset to the community...which is poised to let her down....

His great grandfather once posed here for a photograph capturing him and his restaurant at a time when all of this was awake and alive. Now, standing in the same spot, none of it was the same...not all of it was lost, but barely awake...and barely alive....

Lighting another cigarette, he exhaled a plume of smoke that snaked around his head as he wiped something wet from the corner of his right eye and noticed that there were very few reddish hues this year – among the trees, that is.

(As Forlorn as)
Children Lost In the Woods

When you stand in front of me and look at me, what do you know of the griefs that are in me and what do I know of yours? And if I were to cast myself down before you and weep and tell you, what more would you know about me than you know about hell when someone tells you that it is hot and dreadful? For that reason alone we human beings ought to stand before one another as reverently, as reflectively, as lovingly, as we would before the entrance to hell.

- Franz Kafka, in correspondence with Oskar Pollack,
9 November 1903.

I. "The Green Zone."

So: On Saturday night, the quiet and agreeable cab driver, Dr. Ibrahim Al'Avi, being a refugee of the American occupation of Iraq, began to reconsider his pending U.S. citizenship.

Specifically, he had begun to regret his willingness to a.) accept the refusal of American academia to hire him (his credentials as a behavioural scientist were apparently compromised by his previous collusion with the U.S. military prior to and during the occupation), and b.) accept the advice of an American tourist he had met in a hotel lobby in Baghdad's Green Zone during his last week in his homeland.

"Change yer name," the chubby white man had confided. "You'll never git nowhere in the U.S. with a Mohammedan name like that."

George W. Bush's second term surge had finally stabilized much of the invaded nation by way of bribing sectarian chieftains with bushels of American lucre, and now, though both governments disapproved, here was a bank manager from St. Louis, Missouri, who was touring the Fertile Crescent with his wife and twelve other Free Will Baptists, visiting all the sites that figured into the ancient story of "Father Abraham."

The bank manager's name was Dale.

His wife's name was Mattie.

Their tour (part of a small trend in mostly-American tourism that had recently begun to persist despite vehement warnings that *stability* was not to be mistaken for *safety*) was the "Looking for

Abraham" tour offered through a Christian travel agency in Bible Grove, Illinois, which specialized in escorting handfuls of mostly-white, mostly-Midwestern, mostly-Baptists through war zones to sites where Great Scenes of the Bible had supposedly played out.

The "Looking for Abraham" tour, for example, began in the south at the ruins of Ur, then followed the Euphrates north and west, stopping to admire the former capital of Babylon, and concluding at Harran (Carrhae), in southern Turkey – a total journey of over 770 miles accomplished in three days.

Dale was waiting for his wife to emerge from one of the lobby elevators when Dr. Al'Avi sat down at the bar, two seats removed from the American, and ordered a glass of lemon water...which was precisely what Dale was drinking and all the reason the tourist needed to justify moving a stool closer, thrusting out a smiling, meaty paw of friendship and introducing himself.

"Ibrahim Al'Avi," the quiet Iraqi reciprocated, and Dale's eyes expanded into full moons.

"You mean *A*-bra-*ham*?" the Midwesterner's bright pronunciation bounced and ricocheted through the hotel lobby like a drunken mosquito before coming to rest squarely on the doctor's already-slouching shoulders.

"Yes," he winced.

The American hiccuped with laughter.

"I found you!" he beamed as he pulled a wrinkled itinerary from the hip pocket of his jean shorts. He smoothed the paper clumsily against the side of the bar then set it down for Ibrahim to read. "See?"

Smiling slightly, Ibrahim scanned the page ("A *Torah*-ific Tour!" read the large, bold font at the top of the limp document, which felt as if it had been accidentally laundered in an unchecked pocket), then quietly joked, "I didn't *feel* lost."

Dale hiccup-laughed again.

"Most people don't 'till someone finds 'em," he fortune-cookied as he folded the page back into its origami wad and forced it into a snug pocket. "What brings ya to the lobby oasis, *A*-bra-*ham*?"

Still presenting a slight smile, Ibrahim gestured just as slightly in the general direction of something possibly located in or near the lobby, and which remained unspecified even in speech: "I'm waiting for someone with the right key to open a door for me."

"Who isn't, huh?" Dale muttered wistfully as he tickled a bead of condensation down the side of his glass.

Sipping his own water, Ibrahim's eyebrows bounced involuntarily.

"I wish I was being philosophical," he explained, "but I am literally waiting for someone – anyone – who has a key to Ballroom B to come and unlock the door so that I may begin setting up for my lecture."

Looking at his watch: "Which begins in 45 minutes."

"Yikes, perfesser," the foreigner joked, demurring slightly in the company of someone who, it turned out, actually had business to attend to.

Dale was just waiting for his wife....

"Whatcha speakin' on?" he asked, and Ibrahim suddenly straightened and offered something resembling eye contact to Dale's glass.

"The Connections Between Political Conservatism and One's Sensitivity to Feelings of Disgust," he recited.

"Yikes," repeated Dale, only this time mumbling it to the very same glass his barmate had just addressed.

"Yikes, indeed," added Ibrahim. "I'm a behavioural scientist – my days are *full* of 'yikes' moments."

"Ha!" was the hiccuped reply, then: "Sounds above my pay grade."

"No, no, no," Ibrahim smiled, consoling Dale's sweating glass. "Put simply – there is no physiological difference between the emotional response demonstrated by a toddler when confronted with a new food and that which lies at the heart of many conservative movements."

"Um…"

"Which isn't to say that *every* conservative movement is a reflection of its members' sensitivities to such feelings, only to suggest that *any* conservative movement can likely be traced back to it."

"So Christianity is…"

"Christianity, like the Islamic or Hindu faiths, is not an inherently conservative movement – not in a political sense. It only becomes such when it ceases to be a movement of faith."

"But most Christians are conservative."

"Nevertheless, their conservative-ism isn't so much of a response to God as it is a response to the increasingly engineered environments in which they find themselves."

"But the basic morality of Christianity…"

"*Basic* morality is hard-wired into everyone as a matter of survival – therein lies God. Conservative-ism, by contrast, is a potential response to the perceived moral dilemmas created by living in communities of mixed tribes."

"So I should just move my family someplace remote and do as I please?"

Suddenly, as if orchestrated by Basic Morality herself, both the coiffed, painted wife of the American tourist and a hotel employee with a giant ring of keys emerged from the same *ding!*-ing elevator. Scanning the lobby for her husband, the woman wandered into the center of the space before noticing Dale waving to her from the bar. Meanwhile, the man with the key ring walked casually toward Ballroom B, riffling through the massive, jangling collection of keys of varying sizes, shapes, and colors.

"Ya fergot yer vest!" Mattie announced brightly as she strolled toward the bar and hoisted the bulletproof garment like a trophy, her voice bouncing off the tiled floor like an over-inflated football.

Dale thumped his pale forehead with a freckled hand.

"I knew I was fergettin' somethin'" he stammered, his diminutive bride having strangely transformed his entire demeanor. He got up and met her at the end of the bar, where Mattie (who appeared to have been swallowed by her own vest) nodded to Ibrahim with a wide, white smile.

"Who's yer buddy?" she asked.

"*Ah!* Mattie, *this* is *A*-bra-*ham*!" Dale practically sang the name, anticipating the theatrical gasp he knew his wife could be counted on to deliver.

"We found you!"

And the Americans laughed.

In their bulletproof vests, they laughed.

Ibrahim rose from his stool, smiled pleasantly to Mattie (who was approximately his same height) and said, quietly, "Now I must be lost again."

The laughter simmered as the doctor reached for his briefcase (at which Dale had nervously and obviously glanced a number of times in the course of their exchange), then turned and smiled again at Mattie before asking softly to be excused.

"Oh, certainly," Dale answered, urging his wife aside. "Dr. *A*-bra-*ham* has a lecture to give."

"Oh, well, sure," she beamed. "We're just hopin' to scope out the market b'fore we shuffle off to Babylon."

Nervous laughter.

American are notorious for their nervous laughter.

"Don't let us keep you, doctor," Dale nodded with another meaty handshake...and it was the most sincere expression of good will Dr. Al'Avi had known since his wedding day...and it frustrated him.

He didn't want to like Americans, and, for the most part, he had found dislike, resentment, if not outright hatred very easily maintained, but here was a stranger who, though something of a stereotype, was nonetheless earnest, or seemingly earnest about...well, Ibrahim couldn't quite tell, but it was pleasant. Pleasantly earnest. Earnestly pleasant. Ibrahim had been quietly antagonistic by lying about the subject of his presentation ("The Tendency of Depressed Persons to Assume Responsibility for Unfortunate Outcomes Regardless of Their Roles in Decision-Making" is a soporific snoozefest in contrast to "The Infantile Sensibilities of Conservative Movements"), which was just a jerk thing to do in order to get a rise out of the "goofy American"...only to be met with *earnest pleasantness*.

But then it got worse: Without loosening his grip on the doctor's hand, Dale looked the behavioural scientist square in the eye, his smile persisting, and said, "You ever come to St. Louis, U.S.A., you be sure to find us – Dale and Mattie Bulke – and we'll take ya to a ballgame or somethin', huh?"

Unbelievable.

Nervous laughter and general awkwardness aside, two perfect strangers from thousands of miles away had invited him to be their guest – at home, at a ballgame, it didn't matter, but that the invitation (likely a hollow gesture) was even extended at all, much less with such sincerity...*earnestly pleasant sincerity*...Ibrahim didn't know how to respond.

What he told them, however, was news he had shared with no one, nor had he any intention of telling *anyone* until the day of his departure, if even then, and when he heard the words leave his mouth, he immediately wondered, *Why them?*

He heard himself say, confidentially, "I am moving to America next week."

The Bulkes laughed. Dale winked and clapped the doctor on the shoulder with his free hand while still clinging to Ibrahim's hand with the other.

"That's some seriously short notice there, *A*-bra-*ham*," he said. "Maybe once yer all settled and stuff, huh?"

"Stuff?" Ibrahim echoed quietly (and involuntarily) in confusion.

Then Dale not only leaned in, he pulled the doctor closer, as if to confide secret wisdom: "But seriously, if you're comin' to America, you'll wanna change yer name. You'll never git nowhere in the U.S. with a Mohammedan name like that."

And Ibrahim thought again that, yes, it was okay to not like Americans, the earnest sincerity of the Bulkes having seemed to instantly dissolve into a cheap ruse masking the undercurrent of xenophobia that allowed Dale to feel thoroughly justified in making such a statement...never mind that the statement was true. Outside of Sinbad and Aladdin movies, Americans were terrified of Arabs, which had previously been rooted more in the oil cartel than anything else and which had manifested itself in arms-length tolerance laced with stereotypical sarcasm. Since the attacks in 2001, however, sarcasm had given way to outright paranoia, preemptive strikes, and Nixonian surveillance. The subsequent "War on Terror" (which should have delivered free psychotherapy to the American people, *terror* being a perceived emotion rather than a walking, talking boogie man or people) had resulted in the legalization of cruelty and the justification of global fearmongering. Extremism was answered with extremism and rational thought was thrown to the dogs of reactionary excrement.

But Americans fell for it, and they fell for it for the same reason that Ibrahim had just confided his heretofore unspoken plan – because it was all done so earnestly that it couldn't be questioned...could it?

And if earnest pleasantness can be employed to disguise fear as successfully as earnest fear can be used to justify masked extremism, then who can be earnestly trusted?

"Thank you," smiled Dr. Al'Avi. "I'll remember that."

And now here it was four years later and this quiet and agreeable man had found none of what he had come to America looking for, regretted having moved in the first place, and mourned the loss of his identity and status.

He was no longer Dr. Ibrahim Al'Avi, researcher and professor of behavioural science.

He was Johnny Alavi, taxi cab driver.

When Myrtle Henduck climbed into his backseat on Saturday night, however, she called him "Haji."

II. "The Xanadu."

"Take me home, Haji," barked Myrtle as she wrestled her enormous derriere into the backseat of Johnny Alavi's cab, "and don't gimme no lip."

"Of course," he said, reaching for the meter, "and where…"

"I said *zip it*, Saleem!"

And "zip it" he did as he pulled the old Ford Taurus away from the curb and drove north (though Myrtle's house was east).

He had been dispatched to the Hubbard Civic Center (a late 1930s movie house that had been in a constantly alternating state of renovation and decay since the city had acquired it in 1995, when the multiplex cinema was built out by the interstate) and told to wait for Mrs. Henduck, who had apparently suffered some sort of tragedy in the midst of that nights season premiere performance of the community orchestra. Certainly, when he pulled up in front of the flickering neon billboard (the words *Xanadu Theater* reduced to *Xanu Tea*), the modest, murmuring crowd huddled on the sidewalk seemed to suggest that *something* was afoot.

Minutes later, an ambulance pulled up behind him.

More patrons emerged from inside to join the sidewalk discussion.

Johnny rolled down all four windows to listen in, but only caught fragments:

"He seemed okay at intermission."

"Such a good man."

"You shoulda seen the smile on his face."

"Myrtle sure seems pissed."

At which point the car door opened and there was the full-figured Myrtle Henduck being helped into the backseat by Olive Pyatt, the city librarian.

"Season tickets!" Myrtle shouted over her shoulder as she attempted to enter the cab head-and-shoulders first, but could find nothing substantial enough to hold for leverage to pull the rest of herself in. Backing up to attempt an alternate approach, she nailed Olive's left big toe with the heel of her right shoe and the skinny librarian let out a *yelp* that prompted embarrassed giggles from the growing crowd behind her.

Myrtle's pastor, the Rev. Bruce Tassel, stepped forward, seeming to have appeared out of nowhere (no one remembered seeing him at the concert), and touched Myrtle's elbow as she tumbled off of Olive's toe, frightening her, and she pivoted and swung her purse at where she imagined a head might be.

"Back off!" she shouted. "I'm packin' mace!"

And *everyone* backed up, even the breathless Olive, but none faster than the Reverend Tassel, who, fifteen years earlier, having just entered the ministry, had been maced by a parishioner in Springfield, where he had been serving as pastor for only a few months. Attending a Memorial Day service at the cemetery, he had spotted one of his Third Pew Widows kneeling at her husband's grave, pulling weeds from around the base of the stone. But when the Reverend came up behind her without speaking and knelt down to ask if he could help, he spooked her and the old woman spun round on her knees, spraying mace and shouting, "Too close! Too close!"

Now, with his hands over his face, the Rev. Tassel practically ran away as Myrtle turned again and approached the backseat butt-first, her eyes now regarding the glass front doors of the old theatre, through which the paramedics suddenly emerged with their gurney and the shrouded, lifeless body of Myrtle's husband, Myron, which bounced as the wheels navigated the metal doorstop.

"Selfish!" she shouted at the bouncing corpse. "Selfish!" She pointed and followed the gurney with her extended sausage of a finger as she turned to Olive (who was leaning against a nearby fireplug, her left shoe off, and massaging her left big toe) and shouted, "This is the *third* selfish thing he's done today!"

Olive shot Myrtle a stern look of disapproval, but the effect was minimal as Olive's general demeanor was one of stern disapproval, anyway….

Stern Disapproval: Five years earlier, the skeletal spinster Pyatt had been the organizing force behind a movement to oust from office the former mayor, C.J. Bock, who had published a scrawny memoir in which he not only outed himself as a celibate gay man, but described his interaction with the City Council in terms of a lengthy (and, admittedly, unfunny) joke in which a boy who loves clowns winds up being forcibly "loved" *by* a clown. Olive, having been a member of the City Council since Magna Carta, was, of course, offended and banned the book from her library. Apparently omniscient, omnipotent, and omnipresent, she also somehow arranged for his expulsion from the church they both attended and anticipated the combined scandal leading to his resignation as mayor. She even openly groomed the overtly hairy Dick Leslie (President of the Hubbard CrimeCrunchers – a citizens' organization ideally formed to "crunch crime," obviously, and "keep Hubbard safe," but which was, in truth, an anaemic justification for gossipmongering) as C.J.'s mid-term replacement.

Two years later, when informed of the former mayor's attempted suicide, she reportedly clucked her tongue, shook her head, and voiced hope that he wouldn't let failure prevent him from trying again.

III. "The Crawl Space."

His eyes closed, his hands folded in his lap, a smile serenely stretched across his sagging face, Myron Henduck's eighty-eight year old heart had slowed to a stop as he imagined the slithery ballerina of Ravel's *Bolero* kicking high and twirling through the smoky haze of a French cabaret, caressing empty chairs, sprawling her arms and torso across every other table and establishing such intense eye contact with her exclusively male audience that each patron felt blest. Somehow, the knowing smiles reflected back to her evoked ancient, secret histories, though she had only just begun her dance and scarcely lingered near any man long enough to afford more than the brevity of shared breathing space as she twirled now toward the center of the room, where the spotlight was and where she was free to dance exquisitely as the sole focus of everything until....

In all fairness, and though he had literally spent most of it on his back, it had been a long day for Myron. His obese, blushing bride of sixty-six years had clogged the pipes (again) and when neither the plunger nor the toilet snake could move the offending occlusion, it became clear that Myron (being the thinner Yang to Myrtle's fulsome Yin) had no choice but to spelunk beneath the house...again.

In fact, there was nary a year of their marriage wherein Myron hadn't had to crawl beneath their modest, hastily built home a number of times to access the pipe under the toilet – a long and arduous crawl to the center of the house for the occasional handyman who was unfamiliar with the terrain of the three foot gap between the joist and the earth (called in *only* because Myron was at work or if the task clearly required more than Myron's two hands...as in June, 1968; May, 1975; November, 1983; August, 1989; March, 1999; and July, 2003); for Myron, however, it was an easy trek into well-charted territory that generally presented little by way of surprise....

Sure, it was dark, and it was squishy, and the spiders still sent a prepubescent chill through his octogenarian body, but aside from the occasional spooked possum (as in March, 1959; February, 1960; April, 1967; February, 1973; March, 1979; April, 1982, and so on...) Myron was proud that he could still scurry through the space on his elbows and knees, like a paratrooper under barbed wire, and skillfully dodge every ancient rock or dead tree root that remained jutting from the soil. After sixty-six years of such missions, he had essentially carved a small, twisting trough to the afflicted plumbing, often resulting in a journey through cold, standing water, but which steered the keen adventurer clean of all low-hanging pipes, nail snags, and jagged Nature.

Jagged Nature: Begun in 1945 in response to the modest oil boom that had brought the Kagy Oil Company to the northeastern quarter of the county (where millennia of critters had apparently laid down, died, and liquefied), the Hanley Creek sub-division, of which the Henduck mansion was a part, had been quickly planned and poorly constructed to accommodate the households who accompanied the workmen hired to establish and maintain the twenty-seven pumps that came to dot the farms and woods in the immediate vicinity. For largely unexplained reasons, however, the planners planned the sub-division along a previously unimproved stretch of the Hanley floodplain that was barely 500 feet wide and rose to only twelve feet before leveling off just next to the county highway. Here, the narrow, four foot deep creek made a gentle turn true south in its otherwise southeasterly descent from the higher ground of Daily Township (where the creek began as a natural spring atop the hill that was the old Missionary Baptist cemetery), but here, also, flash flooding had always regularly occurred. Indeed, such had always been the very reason why the original owners of the land (the Spitsingers) had never cleared or used the spot, though the rest of the surrounding parcel had once been quite actively (if not exhaustively) farmed. Nevertheless, here was where an army of contractors descended in the last days of World War Two to clear the soggy, sloping land, lay down streets, and within a mere three years, created a working class neighborhood of ten small, flimsy houses, only seven of which remained (and only five of which were occupied) in the last days of Myron Henduck.

Jagged Nature: Beneath Myron's house (and in sharp contrast to the tiny-but-perfect lawn that he had proudly maintained throughout his tenure there), the floodplain remained as the backhoe had left it – uneven and squishy, the loam of countless ice ages turned over and over in the process of pulling trees and cutting roots...all soil is ancient, but Myron, who had been Kagy's on-site geologist, perceived something of Pangaea in his scurrying beneath the house and sometimes, weather permitting, he would even actually linger in the artificial cavern and imagine the goo between his fingers as contact with that pre-human epoch, when his yard lay at the bottom of a shallow inland sea at the Equator....

Jagged Nature: The Hanley Creek sub-division was built on both sides of a single semi-circular street (Spitsinger Street), which descended from the county highway and curved back six feet from the edge of the creek...which was where the Henduck house stood and where, because the creek was spring-fed and because it passed through two townships of smaller adjacent creeks and drainages, the water table was *always* high. In addition, the large feeder pipe that serviced the sewage needs of the Henduck's side of the street connected to the "main stem" beneath the side yard, where the deep and extensive root system of a three foot tall Oak stump continued to hold the creek bank in place while also compromising the local effectiveness of the entire system...a problem that always first manifested itself in the Henduck's water closet, where the toilet would swirl and spill....

Squishy floodplain aside, however, the most clear and common affliction confounding the pipes beneath the Henduck house was Myrtle's bowels, which hadn't worked properly since she was a tiny, little girl.

Indeed, once upon a time, as a tiny, little girl, Myrtle had been so unreasonably disgusted with the natural functions of her own body that she would literally go to great pains to avoid indulging them.

At the age of seven, she had doubled-over in pain and tears at her sister's ninth birthday party as her innocent bladder protested its swollen condition (36 hours of liquid waste having pushed the unsuspecting organ to its limit) and, as she hit the floor, released an acrid stream of urine that spread quickly across the wood floor of her parents' farmhouse, soaking both her dress and the braided rug beneath the supper table.

Her sister and cousins ran from the room screaming, their little hands in the air as if in military surrender.

Mr. Clemens, their geriatric golden retriever, heard the ruckus and sauntered into the room, crossed the floor to where Myrtle lay crying, sniffed the nearby rug, and vomited.

"Myrtle pissed her dress!" her sister announced at the top of her lungs as their mother emerged from the kitchen, the cake in her hands, and pushed through the frantic exodus to find her soggy, weeping daughter curled up on the floor.

"Dammit, Myrtle!" she sputtered. "I'll *never* get that rug aired out!"

And she never did. Wash followed wash followed wash, but the rug inevitably dried to emanate the same potent mix of concentrated urine and regurgitated dog chow....

Six years later, her uncle Charlie, who was Chief Surgeon at the Catholic hospital, took radioactive pictures of her swollen abdomen and pelvis and discovered that the pubescent lass, having persistently refused the call to evacuate her bowels, had stretched her intestines (already almost twenty feet in length) into a conjugated mass of bulging segments wherein, speculated Uncle Doctor Charlie, the nerves and muscles were likely so damaged that any or all natural urge to move her bowels was faint, if real at all.

"Right?" Charlie quizzed his niece, who nodded her sad and guilty agreement.

So the question was: *X-ray, x-ray on the wall,*
   are Myrtle's bowels functional?

And the answer was: *Yes, of course, to some extent,*
   though she will always harbor excrement....

...which was to say that Myrtle was doomed to spend every weekend of the rest of her life enslaved to the capricious dog whistles of laxatives and stool softeners, bran muffins and hot tea. A short, invisible chain kept her in close proximity to the lavatory wherever she was (mostly, at home) and seriously limited her social options as a wife and mother. At church, she and her family were likewise found to occupy the back pew closest the Ladies Room (which, at times, still wasn't quite close enough), and she knew (she *knew*) that despite decades of unswerving service to the congregation as church secretary there were those who fancied her back-benching as a manifestation of small faith....

But it was no small faith that had kept the personally lithe Myron diving beneath the house for 66 years. To the contrary, he had adored Myrtle since a midsummer church mixer had introduced them to each other 73 years earlier (conspired into existence by the respective parents of the Hubbard Campbellite Church and the Spring Arbor Campbellite Church, which worshiped ten miles northeast of town near the unincorporated farming village of Ellis)...and while Myrtle had actually preferred the attentions of Randy Pankey, whose father owned the Spring Arbor sawmill...the farmer's boy, Myron Henduck, had come home from Korea first (a panic attack during drills at Fort Leonard Wood brought new attention to a heart murmur that had somehow missed detection during his entrance physical; when Randy Pankey came home a year later, he brought his Korean wife and child with him…)…and Myron was just *so keen*….

Approaching the afflicted pipe, he squirmed, then wriggled onto his side, then contorted himself likewise again onto his back before using his heels to push himself closer…and closer…until he was directly beneath the toilet and the pipe, old and iron, which made a turn to the south just above Myron's head and connected to a larger pipe several feet away. Here, he paused as he heard the telephone ring overhead, inside the house, followed by the prompt and heavy *thump, thump, thump* of Myrtle's feet as she moved hurriedly and deliberately through the house in search of the cordless device.

"*Tweedle-eedle-eedle-eedle-ee!*" chirped the phone.

"Dammit!" complained his bride as she smacked some part of her body on sturdy furniture.

"*Tweedle-eedle-eedle-eedle-ee!*"

He heard a book (?) fall and another expletive rise, and for 2.7 seconds he thought he felt the slightest prod of passé shame for "listening in" – a fleeting sensation of adolescent sheepishness that nudged him like an arthritic finger as his mother's voice quietly escaped from behind his eardrums and evoked three generations of disgruntled sopranos.

"Quit yer listenin'!" he heard his mother demand in a stern-but-girlish whisper, as when, as a boy, he would become too quiet around adults.

Then his wife: "Hello?...Kathleen…."

It was their daughter, 43 years old, who called faithfully from her dysfunctional home in Elkhart, Indiana, every third Saturday of the month, whether she needed anything from them or not (though she generally called seeking *something*, be it gossip, advice, a relic from the attic, money)….

He imagined he could recite the usual *blah-de-blah* of their conversation: the Prologue of pleasantries and weather reports; the First Act, consisting of summaries of respective activities (the mundane misadventures of their twin grandsons; a recounting of his and Myrtle's trip to the orchard north of town for a new jar of jam); the Second Act, being the "The Ask" (for gossip, advice, a relic, money); the Third Act, wherein an argument ensues based on the subject(s) of the previous Act; and the Epilogue, in which most was resolved for another month and pleasantries resumed...he imagined it according to the muffled, rumbling cues of Myrtle's voice through the floorboards as he fitted the wrench around the pipe (just above the elbow joint) and *pushed*...

...and *pushed*...

...and *pushed* as his biceps became an angry chorus of displeasure and his face reddened in frustration, his eyes swelling with tears.

Protein shakes be damned!, he thought, perceiving himself duped by the aesthetic that was his own body, which remained thin and comparatively firm (which his doctor had praised just days earlier), but which was still *old*.

"God *bless* it!" he fumed as he pushed against the handle, his palms feeling like fire, and the wrench turned slowly with great resistance, but the pipe (old and iron) stayed still, unmoved, stubborn.

Stubborn: He stopped and silently glowered, the irony of modern "conveniences" having entombed him yet again, as the conversation overhead again commanded his attention, suddenly involving him in the third person.

"Your father?" he heard Myrtle intone, repeating their daughters long-distance cue. "He's under the house again."

He chuckled to himself ("*Again,*" he muttered) and re-positioned the wrench...

("Yes, dear," Myrtle half-sang, half-sighed, "*underneath the house.*")

...and he tightened his grip.

"I know it's hot outside," the Love of His Life allowed, a defensive clause percolating behind her dentures, "but your father..."

He took a deep breath...

("Kathleen...*Kathleen*...Kath-*leen!*")

...and he pushed against the wrench, his face puckering and reddening, his heartbeat *leaping* into his ears...

("Dammit, Kathleen!")

...and his burning hands slipped, sending the tool thudding to the dirt and a thousand cobwebs flying.

"Your *father* is not a *child!*"

And yet, at that moment, he was exactly that – a fuming, flailing adolescent, his heels digging deep into the shadowy squish of the crawlspace as his fingers tightened and curled into bitter fists that swung at the pipe, *pounded* the elbow joint, and caused the entire system of plumbing to shudder above him.

"Mother-lovin' piece of..." he grunted through clenched jaws, his soft teeth grinding as he took up the fallen wrench, wielding it as a warrior's sword, and slashed through the minimal space to bring it *clanging* against the pipe, *clanging* against the pipe, like an angry, industrial church bell decrying the faith it served.

Clanging against the pipe...something broke loose and his face was instantly awash in an unholy spritz of sewage that sprang from just above the elbow joint and descended to blind him and filled his nose and mouth with the unspeakable.

He scrambled, he squirmed, he twisted like a psychedelic inchworm, clawing the dirt and gagging as he turned on his side and wriggled away from the assault....

Gagging and squirming, it was, to him, suddenly very hot and very close under the house, and fear swept over him like the blast from a freshly stoked bonfire....

Gagging and twisting (almost convulsing) he was quickly and quite thoroughly terrified....

It was practically three miles before any words seasoned the atmosphere of Johnny Alavi's cab.

Three miles...and the trees turned into woods....

He heard the widow Henduck sniffle, then stir, then he glimpsed her in the rear view mirror as she wiped something from her eyes....

Sniffling and stirring, Myrtle looked out at the passing landscape for the first time since leaving the Xanadu....

The passing landscape...*the trees had turned into woods!*

"This is the wrong way," she mumbled, her broad alto now a quiet, clenched gurgle.

Defeated, she practically whispered, "This is the wrong damn way."

IV. "The Backseat."

Suddenly, Myrtle felt a rumbling in her abdomen that betokened the lingering influence of a certain laxative, followed by a squirting sound that was clearly audible as a stretch of her intestine gurgled to life and sent a simultaneous message of undeniable urgency to the freshly-minted widow's ancient sphincter and brain, both of which twitched in response.

"Turn right here," she blurted and Johnny Alavi's posture went rigid as he applied the brake.

"Where?"

"Here."

"This is a driveway."

"No, I mean the road."

"Green Road?"

"Yes!"

And although the over-educated cabbie executed a quick, but safe and flawless right turn that was barely detectable inside the automobile itself, the momentary shifting of weight brought more silent tears as another rumble and squirt underscored the backseat emergency and Myrtle winced, cradled her middle torso, and suppressed a whimper.

O Lord, she thought, *it's nearly five miles to home now...and this fool is driving the speed limit!*

O Lord....

Her prayer was impromptu and unlike any she had previously conjured, aloud or in contemplation, but she was a swirl of conflicting emotions – each one vying for dominant consideration – and now....

She closed her eyes and furrowed her brow as she imagined her Creator and urgently, but silently, addressed Him through the boiling fog of the last ninety minutes....

Meanwhile, the road inclined to become a bridge, carrying her over Warner Creek and the Union Pacific tracks that snaked through the floodplain....

As a girl, she had always visualized her God as a combination of her father and Burl Ives – kindly, bearded, sturdy, and capable of sound as perfect as refracted light, illuminating her dreams with a chorus of seventy identical voices singing in unison, the song swirling round her head before bending into her ears as one voice, answering her childish fears with a warming comfort that was neither "yes" nor "no" nor even "wait," but the promise that "this world will lose its motion, dear, 'fore I prove false to thee."

But men are not God (*duh!*), and once her father was mingled with dust her visualization focused on Myron, who was neither bearded nor sturdy, nor able to sing, but nonetheless kindly and possessed of a baritone that rumbled from his chest and greeted the humidity with authoritative incongruity – the wiry bookworm, suspected by new acquaintances of being a mealy tenor, was a rotund baritone who could make even the dullest of ears twitch in unexpected re-discovery of the sound of their native tongue.

In Myrtle's dreams, God became an echo of the sound of her husband's voice as she heard it when reclined against him, her ear pressed to his chest and his "I love you" resonating in harmony with his breath and underscored by the fleshy drumbeat of his heart.

But now...now, as she silently invoked her Saviour's name and muttered a quiet "Amen," she could conjure no voice to answer hers, seemed to sense her world had stopped, felt abandoned in the ensuing vacuum....

Her gut twisted again and suddenly she was weeping openly.

Only hours earlier, Myron had wondered aloud if it was wise to attend the orchestra, given her usual weekend cleanse. But of the adjectives orbiting Myrtle's persona, "reasonable" was not among them; she knew her mind and the contents thereof were not open to interpretation. "Stubborn" and "difficult" were also among the satellites circling Myrtle, as was "awful" (courtesy of Kathleen), but so were "brilliant" and "wonderful," courtesy of Myron, who saw only confidence in his wife's demeanor and found it endlessly attractive.

"I'll not be a hostage," she had demanded and he had demurred, but now...*Dammit,* she thought, *he was right.*

"Mrs. Henduck?"

She heard the cabbie's voice float back to her over the seat that divided them.

"Mrs. Henduck?"

And she heard it again – a gently drifting intonation of her married name.

Her married name.

"Mrs. Henduck, where precisely am I going, please?"

She grimaced and turned to the window, squinted at the darkness, but saw only her own faint reflection – bereft, angry, and on the verge of shitting herself.

"Have we bridged the tracks?"

"Yes, ma'am."

"Fork in the road?"

"No, ma'am."

"At the fork, keep left."

And on cue the taxi's headlights revealed a surprisingly sharp forking of the road that jutted out of the darkness like the bow of a ship in a thick fog.

"Right!" the cabbie blurted affirmatively, his spine stiffening and his adrenaline instantly answering the call of perceived danger as he steered the car left onto a gravel and dirt track that just as instantly deteriorated into dips and holes that bounced the entire vehicle violently before he was able to slow to a vital crawl.

"No!" Myrtle practically shrieked as she clutched her stomach, clamped her eyes shut and clinched every muscle in her body against the bounce and thud of the slowing car (though not slowing fast enough…). "I said left!"

"Woman, I *have* turned left!" the cabbie blurted again, his voice now seasoned with an impatience he had, admittedly, earned and punctuated by the violent vibrato of the bouncing car.

And the car shuddered and rattled as the potholes gave way to trenches – deep grooves of crusty mud that paralleled a grassy hump that rose sharply and threatened the entire exhaust system of the economy sedan as it scraped and bounced and scraped and bounced before stopping abruptly.

Myrtle gritted her teeth and moaned as the laws of physics pushed her slightly forward and then suddenly back in response to the cabbie's unexpected slamming of the brakes...but there was a house....

A house in the middle of the road.

Annoyed, the cabbie, Johnny Alavi (Dr. Ibrahim Al'Avi), threw the gear shift into "Park," undid his seat belt, turned to face his passenger and, with measured patience, demanded to know where they were and why.

But Myrtle was scrambling.

Scrambling and crying.

"Help me out of here!" she wept as she pawed at the door handle, pushed the door open, then squirmed to lift her right leg out of the car.

"*Help me!*" she begged again before stopping, cradling herself and moaning into the fraught darkness that lay beyond the reach of the cab's dome light.

"Oh my God," she moaned in genuine prayer that quickly crumbled into desperate whisper, "help me...."

VI. "The Headlights."

Although it had only taken him seconds to rush around to Myrtle's door, by the time the doctor/cabbie got there he found that she had managed to get both legs out of the car and now sat facing out, but otherwise motionless, her head down and her hands in her lap.

"Mrs. Henduck?" he murmured as he knelt in front of her.

Slowly, she raised her head to greet his shadowed gaze with that of her own, then sniffled, took a deep breath, and spoke her apology with as much dignity as she could muster.

"I'm so sorry, Ravi," she sputtered, her voice quivering, "but I've just…."

Her voice evaporated as the smell suddenly rode a light breeze and delivered itself to olfactory judgment.

"Oh!" he blurted, recoiling to his feet and holding out his hands. "Let's deliver you from this."

And together, Myrtle and her cabbie stepped away from the car, holding hands and silhouetted against the high beams that were focused on the unexpected house confronting them.

"Where are we, Mrs. Henduck?" he now asked quietly, gesturing to the house though the old lady's gaze remained downcast, her head hanging low, her shoulders locked in a hunch.

Framing their silhouettes, the old house was likewise locked in what appeared to be the final throes of resistance to its own circumstances – long-abandoned, the once sturdy, two-story, Federalist-style frame structure seemed to sag between its apparently still-sturdy corners. In the headlights of the cab, loose plaster and wiring could be seen through the open front door, dangling like ganglia. Without glass, the windows were like deep, open sores and the rain damage that stained the formerly white plank siding was blackened with wood rot, lending each sore the appearance of oozing....

"Mrs. Henduck..." His voice now betokened infinite patience, and perhaps it was that very quality that brought her soft, tired eyes up to meet his, but he could now also see the squirm of mixed emotions on her face – the profound loss, the embarrassment, the anger....

He could also see that she desperately needed a tissue.

"Your name isn't Ravi, is it?" she gurgled quietly, a snot bubble inflating under her right nostril as her cabbie retrieved a travel packet of Tender Touch Tissues from the front passenger seat.

"No," he smiled, handing her the packet. "Neither is Haji nor Saleem."

The old woman blew her nose and let loose a gurgled chuckle that was as much of a sob as any other noise that had escaped her in the last hour.

"Sorry I'm such a bitch," she mumbled, wiping her nose.

The cabbie clucked his tongue and shook his head – a useless non-vocal cue in the dark.

"I don't think you're that, Mrs. Henduck," he said preparing to qualify his statement by reminding her of her immediate loss, but was stopped by another gurgle/sob.

"Suddenly, I'm not even 'Mrs. Henduck' anymore," she mourned, somehow intoning the inverted commas around her married name.

The sentence hung in the air as they stood silently...oblivious to the movement visible through an illuminated and otherwise empty second floor window of the abandoned house.

In the glow of the cabs headlights, something moved and watched....

VI. "The Darkness."

He almost told her everything.

That is, he almost made the very same mistake with Myrtle that he had made years before with the Bulkes in a hotel lobby in Baghdad's Green Zone.

He almost told her too much.

Starting with his name, his family, his credentials and continuing through to his co-operation with the U.S. military...co-operation that secured his family's safe evacuation out of Iraq and to the middle of the United States, where tentative citizenship awaited his wife and children.

Co-operation his wife had never supported nor respected.

She didn't want evacuation.

She called him a coward.

Angrily, she called him a coward.

As a respected social scientist at the University of Baghdad, he had been quietly approached by the U.S. government before the invasion – "We want to understand all possible contingencies before we break this," the visitor had said, gesturing around Ibrahim's office to signify the country as a whole.

But when approached later by generals in desert fatigues, it wasn't for insight into the character or spirit of the modern Iraqi, nor for counsel regarding human behaviour, in general. The generals came seeking advice and comment on the potential long term effects of interrogation practices at a nearby prison where many of his fellow countrymen, confused by dogma or in thrall to a charismatic cleric, were being held and humiliated.

How far can we go before…?

The generals sought parameters, justifications, permissions…not insight.

And the generals asked him to stay, to tarry in consultation for what dragged into three years….

Three years, it turned out, was all his family needed to disappear completely….

He had tried to keep in touch – he had provided his wife and oldest daughter with temporary cell phones and discreet e-mail address, and for several weeks after their departure from Baghdad and arrival in the U.S. there were numerous telephone conversations and electronic dispatches, each one an uneven mix of fear and longing, indignation and apology, but were nonetheless *contact*.

However…as the days piled up and turned into weeks, months, and years, the contact became less frequent, more strained, increasingly impatient and angry until the calls ended altogether and e-mails remained unanswered. By the time he was finally given leave to join his family in the U.S., he felt he had withered into a silhouette of a human – his form as a man was roughly accurate, but no details were discernible. He was nameless and adrift with no country, no work, and now no family….

They had been here – his wife's cousin practiced geriatric medicine at the Catholic hospital and had agreed to receive her and their children upon their arrival in the U.S. as "resident aliens." The two

families had even lived together for some eighteen months before he
had lost contact.

Before contact was severed.

He had hoped for a reunion, a position at an American
university, a continuation of the stability and sweetness that had defined
their lives before the occupation...he had passed a great deal of time
romanticizing the near future, anticipating a cinematic version of his
increasingly rose-tinted memories....

But the cousin wasn't talking. Not about Ibrahim's family. He
knew exactly where they were and why they had moved on without
waiting, but he had also promised not to share the information.

He was sorry, but he had promised.

But Ibrahim had made promises, too. He was noble, too. That
others lacked the patience to allow him to keep those promises....

So he stayed. He gave up on academia, took odd jobs to pay
bills, and dug in for the long haul, waiting in Hubbard in the hopes (the
off chance) that his family might return. For whatever reason. And that
he might find them when they did.

When they do.

He almost told Myrtle everything, and for a split second the
urge to do so was practically irresistible, the words lingering on the
back of his tongue like a pungent spice.

Standing in the headlights of his cab, however, and holding
hands with the sobbing widow, he felt that the surrounding darkness and
the ruined farmhouse that gaped lifelessly at the incongruous duo

discouraged any such disclosure. *This is her sadness*, he thought instead. *Her darkness*.

So he stood silently, holding her hands, and waited as Myrtle delivered her pain to the cool, humid summer air....

❧

"I own this land," she finally said, having discovered an island of calm in the midst of her loss. Releasing the cabbie's hands, she wiped her eyes and nose and stood fully erect for the first time since exiting the car. "Somehow, I'm the last of my family; no one else survives...and once I'm gone...."

She paused and thought of her daughter, Kathleen, who ran from home as fast as her skinny, rebellious legs could carry her once she was a legal adult. For reasons both real and imagined, she couldn't put enough distance between herself and the town that had produced her, or the family who had nurtured her...this land meant nothing to her. Adrift and disconsolate in her Thirties, Kathleen had once given in and come home for a potential "reboot" (which failed) and when Myrtle brought her here and showed her the bulk of her potential inheritance, the prodigal declared it nothing but a looming tax burden and dismissed the entire concept of being tied down to a single piece of land.

"At every turn, she's broken my heart," Myrtle sniffled, "and I bounce between anger and sadness over it, but she's her mother's daughter...simply won't be told...."

She turned to face the old house and her over-educated cabbie followed suit.

"This is your childhood home?" he asked.

"No," she said, sounding disappointed. "Our house was on the other side of this parcel. This was where my Uncle Raymond and Aunt Bertie lived."

She stepped toward the structure just a step or two, but enough that Johnny Alavi was at last able to see and evaluate the extent of Myrtle's backseat accident – the back of her dress was a dark smear, as was the backseat where she had previously been seated. As he moved to retrieve the blanket he kept in the trunk (for emergencies – the winters here were cold and if the Taurus broke down in the middle of nowhere…), his disheveled passenger continued.

"They never had children," she said, speaking over her shoulder as she surveyed the ruined house, "so they lavished attention on me and my sisters. Spoiled us the way our grandparents would have if they had been alive. I particularly loved Bertie, who was so kind to me…." Her voice trailed off as the cabbie returned and wrapped a folded blanket around her shoulders.

"Thank you," she said, finally managing a meagre smile and turning to face him. "You have any family?"

Again, the academic cabbie felt the urge to unload his story...but to what end? After this, he would deliver her home and likely never interact with her again...but to the extent that he understood self-disclosure to be an act of trust, he knew that she anticipated some level of reciprocation regardless of her actual interest….

"Yes," he said, putting on a broad smile that he hoped would disguise the acute anguish that underscored his reality; the mystery of why he was forsaken. "My wife and three daughters."

"Three daughters," she repeated softly, wistfully envious of his apparent good fortune. Looking back at the house, she instantly recalled coming to stay with Ray and Bertie after her first miscarriage...Myron fuming under his breath as she refused to go home but asked to be brought here instead, where she spent a week in the encouraging embrace of Bertie's doting care. She remembered feeling unprepared to face her own house, where she had spent the last several weeks ebullient in the anticipation of her first child. Sixty years later, the memory still sought to cripple her, more so than even the memory of returning here a year later under the same circumstances, and when the life she had intentionally cultivated to hide herself from the memory failed to serve its purpose and the remembrance of her loss roared at her from the past, she had learned to also re-discover the unquestionable sense of warmth and assurance that had steeled her emotions in the week she spent in this house.

This house...

This decrepit old house....

On paper, she was the owner of all of this, being the only one left, but the farmhouse she had grown up in on the other side of these 320 acres was long gone and she hadn't been out here for forty years.

Not since Bertie died.

That she was suddenly here again on this particular evening was pure coincidence...but wholly appropriate....

And the invisible tennis match continued as Myrtle now turned back to her cabbie, practically snapping her head as if she had just remembered that she had left a candle burning at home, but underscored by a slight smile: "What *is* your name?" she asked in a previously unheard tone of surprising tenderness.

Reflexively, Ibrahim smiled. "Johnny," he said quietly with what he instantly feared to be obvious embarrassment but which Myrtle thankfully perceived as a little joke.

She giggled and wiped her nose. "Is that a common name in...where are you from?"

"I was born in Egypt," he said...and it wasn't a lie: his mother, nine months pregnant, had joined her banker husband in Cairo on a business trip when Ibrahim sought deliverance, ruining brunch for her and her midwife. But he hated the head shaking and tongue clucking that inevitably accompanied the average American response to his identifying as Iraqi ("Shame about your country," was a common refrain that always felt to Ibrahim like a random dependent clause in search of clarification).

Myrtle giggled again. (In the mid-1980s, she and Myron had sponsored an Indonesian orphan through a mission program at church – a child whose name was a string of consonants and vowels that made Myrtle's tongue hurt, but who identified herself in letters as "Jenni.")

She wiped her nose again. (After three years, the now-teen-aged "Jenni" had fallen out of touch with the Henducks on the heels of her conversion to Islam, which Myrtle had taken personally and mourned as if she had lost her own daughter...again....)

"I was born a quarter of a mile that way," she said, pointing into the darkness beyond the old house to her left.

His eyes silently following her finger, he told her that "most of the world dies within a mile of where they were born," but didn't comment on the movement he thought he spied through an upstairs window. Rather, he gently touched her elbow, and urged her toward the front passenger seat of the cab.

"We'll ride as friends," he smiled as she now wrapped the blanket around her waist and began her usual awkward descent onto the car seat.

He glanced back over his shoulder as she grunted and pushed herself into place...what *was* that he had seen? A raccoon? Possum? Some other petulant monster? Before moving to the U.S., he had never known forests or woods like these and the fact that many full grown adults found them terrifying made perfect sense to him.

He leaned in to close the door but stopped short as Myrtle rolled down the window and smiled at him sheepishly.

"I'll pay for whatever it takes to clean up your backseat," she offered, her eyes still soft with burgeoning tears and her voice a wisp of the full-throated alto she had been only minutes earlier.

"Yes," he said, trying to disguise the urgency he now felt as he again glanced over his shoulder at the house. "Yes, that would be very nice."

"You've been so kind to me," she added, almost under her breath as she reflected on her own behaviour this evening...and the loss....

He smiled as he finished the distance and closed Myrtle's door, glanced once more at the house, then hustled round to the driver's side.

The interior of the car still smelled of shit, but was bearable with all the windows down.

He reached for the gear shift and Myrtle placed her hand on top of his.

"Thank you, Johnny" she said quietly, her modest smile expanding only just slightly.

And Dr. Ibrahim (Johnny) Al'Avi (Alavi) practically blushed. "Thank me when you are home and safe," he said as he pulled the car first slightly forward, turning to the right, then backward to the left, rocking the car front and back in a three-point turnabout that blossomed into the shape of an asterisk before the old Taurus was finally facing back the way they came, the house behind them again shrouded in darkness, like a shipwreck, and leaving whatever was hiding inside it to it's own devices....

VI. "The House."

It was Ron.

Ron Colly, huddled in the windowless window, a stack of bent and weary notebooks leaning against his thigh...he saw every second of Myrtle and Johnny Alavi's strange detour, watched the brisk evacuation of the idling car, their awkward hand holding, her sobbing....

Go away, he had thought, *go away*....

But when they did leave, he couldn't help feeling slightly diminished....

He had been there since sundown, having parked just up the road in the parabola shaped driveway of the old Hopewell Methodist Church and walked through the adjacent cemetery and woods to this old house...a favorite spot of his since college days when he and a friend would sneak inside and get high.

They had never come upstairs, though – he was well into his Thirties before he dared venture up the creaking staircase, having come here alone on a whim motivated by nostalgia. And his heart was in his throat the entire length...seventeen steps, each one possessed of a distinctive creak or unique moan of resentment at having been called to their original function again after all these years. The stair halfway up felt particularly soft, and he did his best not to put his full weight on it, but Gravity's a bitch and no matter how he maneuvered it 160 pounds of Ron Colly came pressing down on the wooden riser as he quickly ascended to the next one, which proved only slightly sturdier but spooked him by groaning louder than any before it....

They had discovered this old house during the summer after their freshman year of college (where the church friends had both discovered marijuana). Taking the scenic route to another friend's home, they had kept left at the same fork in the road that had lately delivered Myrtle and Ibrahim...in the daylight, however, the house had seemed less ominous, more sad, and as its abandonment was a more recent event the remains of the lives lived here were more easily identified. Now, thirty years later, however, the soggy and decrepit structure no longer shared any secrets. Rather, peering through the darkness that engulfed him in the wake of Myrtle and Ibrahim's departure, the entire scene seemed devoted to the singular task of teetering – collapse was imminent, but not so long as *this* corner held firm, or *that* beam remained in place. The framers of this house had known exactly what they were doing, and a century later the forces of Nature had yet to prevail against it.

Yet.

Teetering: The stack of notebooks seemed to shift against his thigh, as if to remind him of their existence...*don't forget why you're here*....

He was here for the ritual – the Purging of Memory that had become a recurring, though sporadic feature of his adult life. He had been keeping a journal for 29 years at this point, recording his unsolicited opinions, ideas and aborted inspirations in increasingly haggard notebooks (a mix of spiral bound and glued) that represented an on-going, private conversation with himself about...well...*everything*

– the reservoirs of stimuli that confronted him daily were as bottomless as they often were stupefying.

Stupefying and fascinating.

But there had been a Darkness brewing...all those years, an inherited, anachronistic melancholy had been slowly maturing behind his eyeballs, anticipating the worst in others, quietly suspicious of the world, in general...and when *those* planes ignited *those* fires in New York City....

Not long afterward, he had begun setting fire to old journals. The first batch, written in an evolving script that betokened his waxing ease with words and with writing, covered the years between his tenth and thirteenth birthdays, and they were thick with ideas, observations, jokes, Bible verses...but also clotted with strange anxieties, concerns, doubts, questions, and the growing suspicion that "a lot of people are full of shit."

Especially adults.

He had taken that first batch (approximately thirty notebooks of varying shapes and sizes) into the backyard of the farmhouse he was renting during graduate school, threw them into the trash barrel, doused them in too much lighter fluid, and introduced a flaming match.

"*Fwoooshhhh!*" said his late adolescence as it was instantly translated into curling ash by the fire that engulfed it, the resulting smoke delivering his childhood to the indifferent aether....

And he had instantly felt lighter, but only just.

And how many memories can one destroy without also feeling completely erased?

So the ritual had been a spare occurrence – a catharsis born of necessity whenever the plastic tote became too full of notebooks to get the lid to close properly.

Tonight, the notebooks were 2008 through 2010...and they were evil.

Evil in the sense that they contained, evoked, embodied the Darkness that had consumed him on the heels of loss – an emotional Darkness not unlike the natural darkness of an abandoned farmhouse in the middle of the woods, except nothing in the woods terrified him in quite the same way as the contents of these particular journals.

Here were the things that he had forgotten or repressed...presumably because they were sad...and to the extent that sadness is only thinking...these were the thoughts he had purged, archived, then sequestered to the oblivion of his closet, obscured further from view by a laundry basket full of neatly-folded concert t-shirts.

His subconscious followed suit and when he eventually dared to *try* to conjure a very specific memory from the middle of those two years, he was greeted with Darkness. No flashes of memory, no ghostly shapes or figures bleeding through snowy static, not even a dial tone.

Strange, he thought, *how two full years of existence can devolve into a vacuum....*

All this time, his huddling had been an awkward combination of squatting and leaning against a heavily lacquered end table that had likely been *in situ* since the 1970s, but now he lost his balance and plopped onto his denim derriere with a squish. Like the rest of the house, however, what was left of the shag carpeting was soggy and resentful and allowed no purchase to be gained in his instant scramble back to his feet. He slipped, he slid, he practically pirouetted through the window before coming to a tentative stop, his arms rigid in anticipation of another topple....

Suddenly, the prospect of burning *anything* in the midst of this goo seemed highly unlikely....

But then it occurred to him how the very end table that had previously supported his partial weight was like an altar – a self-assembled altar made of pressed wood chips, but somehow perfect for the purge at hand....

Ron's last accessible memory from 2008: He and The Boy at the gift shop, picking up trinkets for an aunt and cousin who share November birthdays...he has set the child up on the counter top next to him as he signs the credit slip and The Boy turns to smile at the woman whose has just finished wrapping the gifts..."Momma?" he says....

After that, it was a long, slow fade to black that stretched well into 2010...except for the journals he now moved from the floor and balanced atop the table. They were poisonous and deserved their holocaust.

Reaching into his left hip pocket, he retrieved the now-squished and soggy half-empty packet of cigarettes that also contained his lighter...he would have to burn them one at a time; the stack was too big to burn all at once without setting the whole damn house ablaze....

But maybe the house needs purging, too....

Activating the lighter, he noticed a wire hanger just to his right, which he picked up and unwound to slide through the spiral binding of the first notebook – just as he had done as a kid when they roasted wieners in the fireplace at Christmas time....

(He was surprised by how, even though that particular memory had also been burnt in a journal years before, it remained nonetheless accessible...once *these* journals were gone, though....)

His sacrifice held aloft in his left hand (the wire bending and bouncing under the weight of the notebook) he touched it with the flame in his right hand and....

He won't remember any of this.

He will know of the destruction of these journals only by their absence in the tote when he goes to make another purge in five more years, only a small bundle of prose and some verse surviving, clipped together and tucked into the bottom of the container....

He will hypothesize, write, wriggle and contort his approach to the memory multiple times and always find himself at a loss, his access denied. He will picture himself in the third person, imagine entire scenes playing out in new variations of previous speculations, but it's still always just fiction to him.

He will become an old man beneath the house, his bitter widow, her confused and abandoned cab driver, and they will all still end up here...in this old house where Ron sees himself setting fire to the first journal and the flame is an unexpected flare of orange and green that bursts alive and then quickly withers to a seething glow of red.

But the catharsis is missing – that's how Ron knows the memory isn't real. He watches the flames lick their way up the sides of the second notebook and he feels nothing. He remembers the notebook itself, has a flash memory of packing it into an overnight bag, but its translation to ash conjures no feeling.

Neither does he remember leaving the house, much less burning every journal...the "memory" is always two, maybe three notebooks, then fast forward five years and it's "Hey, where's the journals?"

And yet there are other parts of it that are so vivid as to be practically unquestionable...the tangible aspects of being inside the house, the decay, the mouldering smell, the familiarity of the overall loss....

✺

The Overall Loss: Fast forward five years and the house is gone, too.

That is, *he* can't find it.

In an attempt to 'retrace' steps he may very well have only imagined taking in the first place, he has repeatedly driven the length of county road that *should* lead to the fork in the road that *should* become the driveway to where there *should* be a house...but where there is only a clearing in the shape of an amphitheatre, curtained by a thick fabric of trees.

A clearing that is itself overgrown to the point that it illustrates far more than five years.

Overgrown and shaded on a sunny day.

No sign of it ever having been occupied at all.

No evidence that any of it was ever even real.

- August, 2013/August, 2018.

About the Author

According to his submitted biography in Totten's *Who's Who of Fictitious Inkslingers* (Anaesthesia, WI: Totten's House of Promulgation, 2013, Pg. 605), "Dusty Bracken" was the final pseudonym employed by local author Ron Colly following the 2011 loss of his tax exempt status as founder and C.E.P. (Chief Executive Priest) of the American Church of Liberal Piety.com.

His 2010 memoir, *My Friends and Why I Hate Them*, sold 36 copies during its tenure on the shelves of the Covert County Artisan Workshop and Coffee House.

"Ron Colly" is also an alias sometimes employed by Don Jolly in the pursuit of new credit.

Made in the USA
Monee, IL
08 July 2024

61496940R00080